ATLANTIS

LOST

A James Acton Thriller

Also by J. Robert Kennedy

James Acton Thrillers

The Protocol
Brass Monkey
Broken Dove
The Templar's Relic
Flags of Sin
The Arab Fall
The Circle of Eight
The Venice Code
Pompeii's Ghosts
Amazon Burning

The Riddle
Blood Relics
Sins of the Titanic
Saint Peter's Soldiers
The Thirteenth Legion
Raging Sun
Wages of Sin
Wrath of the Gods
The Templar's Revenge
The Nazi's Engineer

Atlantis Lost

Special Agent Dylan Kane Thrillers

Rogue Operator
Containment Failure
Cold Warriors

Death to America
Black Widow
The Agenda

Retribution

Delta Force Unleashed Thrillers

Payback
Infidels

The Lazarus Moment
Kill Chain

Forgotten

Templar Detective Thrillers

The Templar Detective
The Templar Detective and the Parisian Adulteress

Detective Shakespeare Mysteries

Depraved Difference
Tick Tock
The Redeemer

Zander Varga, Vampire Detective

The Turned

ATLANTIS LOST

A James Acton Thriller

J. ROBERT KENNEDY

ISBN-10: 1986839931

ISBN-13: 978-1986839938

First Edition

10 9 8 7 6 5 4 3 2 1

For Stephen Hawking, who revealed more of our world from the confines of a wheelchair, than most throughout history could ever dream.

ATLANTIS LOST

A James Acton Thriller

"But afterwards there occurred violent earthquakes and floods; and in a single day and night of misfortune all your warlike men in a body sank into the earth, and the island of Atlantis in like manner disappeared in the depths of the sea."

Plato, Timaeus, circa 360 BC

"It's a social-validation feedback loop…exactly the kind of thing that a hacker like myself would come up with, because you're exploiting a vulnerability in human psychology…The inventors, creators—it's me, it's Mark [Zuckerberg], it's Kevin Systrom on Instagram, it's all of these people—understood this consciously. And we did it anyway."

Sean Parker, founding president of Facebook
Axios interview, Nov. 9th, 2017

AUTHOR'S NOTE

Please note that this novel, while published the same month the Facebook scandal of March 2018 broke, was written before those events began.

PREFACE

In 2015, 99% of all international data traffic was transmitted over undersea cables, representing an unfathomable amount of information. By 2017, over two billion people had a Facebook account, with the average person having 338 "friends." According to Pew, the average person had actually not even met almost ten percent of those people. Among teenagers, the numbers are even more disturbing, with Pew reporting 57% had made friends online, and less than 20% had met any of those friends in person.

In 2017, Sean Parker, the founding president of Facebook, admitted publicly that social media platforms were intentionally designed to consume the user's time, and one of the methods was to trigger a validation response, designed to reward the user as they spent more of their day on the site. These likes, shares, friend requests, views, messages about a photo or post getting more responses than usual, and other positive reinforcement indicators, were specifically designed to addict the user, forcing them to crave these acknowledgements from people they barely knew, and keep them glued to the platform so the company could make money off them.

This has been admitted publicly.

But will the story be lost in the carefully curated newsfeeds designed to make the users of social media platforms happy?

And what would it take to get a generation that has known nothing but life behind the screen, to wake up, and notice the world around them?

Senate Chambers

Atlantis

Before the fall

"We've heard the stories, yet we still do not heed the warnings. Entire cities wiped out by exploding mountains. Our own scouts have brought back the tales from other civilizations over the centuries, and now that we witness with our own eyes the very same thing happening on our island, we sit and do nothing, denying what is plain to see."

Professor Ampheres strode around the perimeter of the Senate chamber, making eye contact with each and every one of the men and women elected to lead their people. "If we don't start evacuating our people now, we could lose everything our ancestors struggled so hard to build."

The President shook his head, waving his hand. "We will *never* abandon our city. It is all that we are."

Ampheres stared at him as he strode closer to the man who would lead them all to their doom. "The city can be rebuilt, our way of life cannot. If we lose the population, then all that we have built over the centuries will be lost. Our ancestors came here to build a better way of life, and their descendants have succeeded tremendously. Look around you. We live in peace, our population can read and write, our children are educated in math, history, and philosophy, and our architecture is beyond anything imagined elsewhere. Our aqueducts provide us with fresh water, our farms provide us with plentiful food, and our isolation protects us from those who would take it.

"But you've felt the earthquakes, you've seen the steam itself rising from the top of the mountain that dominates our southern sky. What we only recently suspected has now been proven. Our city is built on the side of something that is awakening. If we do not take action now, it could kill us all."

The President leaned forward, staring down at him from his elevated position of honor. "Let us focus on some things you just said. You mentioned our isolation, and how it protects us from our enemies who would take what we have created. It is for this very reason that we can never leave this place. It is the very reason why unapproved travel is strictly prohibited. Our ancestors fled war and constant need, and found this place by accident. It was so isolated, it allowed us to thrive, and by living in peace, and sharing what they had, they built this great civilization, unrivaled in any of the known lands. We tossed off the naiveté of a belief in multiple deities, and that trident, right there"—he leaned to the side, pointing at the artifact that dominated the center of the chamber—"that has sat untouched for centuries, is a constant reminder to us that it is science and knowledge, not superstition, that should guide us.

"Our scientists have said that these earthquakes are nothing to worry about, that they will pass, and that this exploding mountain story you refer to is just that, a story, and that the steam is nothing but water vapor caused by the friction of rocks rubbing together during the quakes. Only *you* seem to think that a calamity is imminent, and that we should ignore all the evidence to the contrary and abandon our civilization. We know from the reports our scouts bring back to us that the lands we abandoned ages ago are still filled with violent primitives. If we were to show up on their shores, what do you think would happen? Do you think they would welcome us with open arms? Or would they treat us as invaders, and slaughter every last one of us? Or would you have us turn into the conquerors of old, and take what we need from those primitives?" The President waved his hand, dismissing everything that had been said. "Professor, your allotted time is up, and I will kindly ask you to leave so the next person can be heard."

Ampheres struggled to control his anger and disbelief at the ignorance and arrogance on display here today. He had little respect for politicians, always having felt they were too often out for themselves rather than the people, but the Senate was the greatest democratic institution known to man, elected every five years by the people in a one person, one vote fashion, and it had proven extremely successful for centuries. That these people would ignore his warnings, and threaten the lives of everyone they had sworn to serve, was infuriating. He jabbed a finger at their so-called leader. "Mr. President, yes indeed, my time is up, but so is all of yours. You, through your ignorance and inaction, have condemned us all to death, and Atlantis to the depths of the ocean that has protected us for so long!"

He spun on his heel and marched toward the doors to the massive chamber, the one hundred men and women elected to rule the island remaining in shocked silence. If any had been swayed by his words, it would appear none were brave enough to let their change of heart be known.

All they care about is reelection.

And his cynicism might be correct. Elections were only six months away, the campaigns had already begun, and with things going so well, nobody wanted to be seen as risking the status quo. He sometimes wondered if their logic was telling them that if he were right, and the island were to be destroyed, then it was better to lose one's life, rather than lose the election if he were wrong.

Disgusting.

While he respected the institutions founded by his ancestors, they had become tired and staid. There were no challenges left. There was no war, no disease, no famine. Their isolation protected them from conflict or the arrival of new diseases, and they wisely stored large amounts of foodstuffs should a harvest fail, or the weather be uncooperative, a rare occurrence in these parts. The population was happy, and any change in their leadership might disrupt that, exploding mountain be damned.

He stared at the trident as he passed it, when an irrational anger swept over him. He strode toward it and grabbed it, the hushed silence surrounding him erupting in a collective gasp as he pulled the surprisingly heavy object from its sacred receptacle. He spun back toward the President, the man's mouth agape, his eyes wide. "You say this is a reminder of the times of old when we worshipped the gods, and how foolish we were. But I say this! *You* have become the new gods, infallible only in your minds, and it is this arrogant belief that you can do no wrong, that will destroy us as surely as any god might have!"

He turned, storming toward the entrance, the trident gripped tightly in his hand, the senators erupting behind him in outrage. And as he cleared the doors, the shocked guards staring at him, not sure what to do, his heart hammered as he realized that no matter what happened over the coming days, eruption or not, he would likely be spending them in a prison cell, forced to watch all that he had known and loved destroyed, powerless to save even his own family.

Off the coast of Pico Island, Azores

Present Day

Sergeant Carl "Niner" Sung pointed toward the seabed, and his diving partner and best friend, Sergeant Jerry "Jimmy Olsen" Hudson gave him a thumbs up then tilted forward as he kicked with his fins, slowly heading for the coral deposits Niner had spotted. They were at almost two hundred feet and approaching the limit with regular tanks. The return to the surface would have to be slow, but the sharp drop off surrounding Pico Island, part of the Azores, an archipelago a thousand miles due west of Portugal, necessitated it if you wanted to see anything truly interesting. Niner was secretly hoping for a shipwreck, or something else manmade, but according to the dive master they had rented the gear from, there wasn't much beyond small personal craft.

No Nazi U-Boats filled with gold here.

But just getting in the water was worth it. If he were forced to describe the sensation, he'd have to say solitary. Despite his friend being only a few yards away, they had no way to communicate beyond hand signals, the water was murky enough to reduce their visibility to a few dozen feet, there was nothing to smell beyond the rubber of his mask, and any sounds were muffled.

And forget about taste—it was overwhelmed by silicone from the mouthpiece his teeth were chomping down on.

As they approached the coral, a smile spread at the myriad of fish swimming around the calcium carbonate deposits left behind over millennia of invertebrates making the formations their homes.

Which came first? The fish or the reef?

He remembered reading somewhere that scientists had settled the age-old chicken or egg debate—the egg of course, since the mutation that created the first chicken would have happened to another creature's egg.

Scientists kill all the fun!

A strange rumbling sound pulsated through the water, and at first, he thought a boat was passing by overhead. He reoriented to look up at the surface above, but could see nothing beyond a general brightness overhead, broken by the gentle ebb and flow of the ocean surface. The rumble continued to grow, and he felt it through his skin as he turned to regain his view of Jimmy. When he finally did, his friend's eyes were wide behind his mask, and he was slowly jabbing his finger toward what should be the shore.

Niner swung his hand, propelling himself around and almost gasped his mouthpiece out as he saw the side of the island, for lack of a better description, sliding deeper underwater, a cloud of dust and debris

10

slowly rolling toward them. He was about to kick his legs to head for the surface when he felt a hand on his arm, and on instinct, he tore it away before realizing it was Jimmy at his side. Niner pointed up and Jimmy shook his head, tapping the gauge indicating their depth. Niner silently cursed, remembering that if they ascended too quickly to the surface, they'd have a wicked case of the bends that could end up killing them if not treated immediately—and he wasn't willing to bet that the Portuguese territory of the Azores had a hyperbaric oxygen chamber that could save them.

Instead, they were forced to slowly kick to the surface and watch the massive landslide taking place in front of them, and pray that any debris that reached them would merely be sand.

I wonder if it could clog our equipment.

They slowly began the controlled rise required for this depth, when the rumble stopped. Niner halted his ascent and floated freely for a few moments as the dirt kicked up by the landslide slowly subsided, gently floating back to the ocean floor. Niner couldn't resist, cutting short his return, and instead cautiously headed for what might be newly revealed ocean floor, treasure of unimaginable value possibly accessible for the first time in decades, or millennia.

As he approached, Jimmy at his side, his eyes played tricks on him. He could pick out shapes in the silt-filled water, shapes that were geometric, straight lines and right angles—manmade, not natural. His heart raced as a smile spread across his face.

It had to be a ship.

He kicked a little harder, Jimmy keeping pace, obviously seeing the same thing. As they neared, the shapes became more distinct, more unnatural, and then suddenly it all snapped into focus. Columns. Buildings. Structures. This was a city, or at least part of one. It stretched out for as far as the eye could see, though that wasn't far. It appeared Greek or Roman to him, but he wasn't the expert.

Hell, it looked like it could have been the Capitol Building for all he knew.

He glanced at Jimmy and gave him an excited thumbs up before they both kicked hard toward the ruins. His heart hammered as if he was in combat, this by far the coolest thing he had ever seen, and he finally understood why Professors Acton and Palmer loved their work so much.

If this is their every day, then my life is just plain boring!

Something glinted below them and he pointed, kicking hard to reach it first, Jimmy beginning to overtake him. He reached out and shoved his friend aside, grasping the exposed piece of metal with his other hand.

Ha!

His friend flipped him the bird, circling around to face him as he struggled to pull from the seabed whatever it was he had found. Jimmy reached out and grabbed another part of the perhaps foot long pole, and together they both yanked, much of their leverage lost to the buoyancy of the water. It finally began to give, and within moments, what looked to Niner to be a honkin' huge dinner fork was revealed, and he suddenly felt like he was in the land of the giants. He glanced

12

over his shoulder to make sure none approached. He held it up in front of him, staring at it, trying to make sense of the encrusted "fork," about six feet in length.

Wait a minute, I know what this is! It's a trident!

He wanted to shout out his revelation to Jimmy, but it was impossible. Jimmy reached forward and scraped at the surface of the object, a general glint of metal coming through, though with so much of the surface covered, it was hard to tell what they had discovered, except that it was quite heavy, even in the water. Niner's eyes widened at what was revealed.

If that's not gold, then I don't know what is!

He pointed up, and Jimmy nodded, there no doubt in his mind who needed to be informed of what they had just discovered.

Outside the Senate Chambers

Atlantis

Before the fall

Ampheres emerged into the bright afternoon sun, the breeze off the ocean light but welcome, the scent of the sea something he would never tire of. To his right, the source of their impending destruction continued to smolder, steam or some other gas wafting into the clear sky like a lazy cloud.

"Professor Ampheres, do you have anything to say to the press?"

"What was it that was so urgent you were granted an audience?"

Ampheres frowned, forgetting what was awaiting him on the steps of the Senate. He was about to open his mouth when someone finally noticed what was still gripped in his hand.

"Is that Poseidon's Trident?"

He stared at it for a moment, unsure of what to do, but quickly realizing that his future of imprisonment was already certain. And he might only have moments to warn the population. He raised the trident in the air, the gathered reporters falling silent. "I have taken this symbol of our past, to remind our present leaders of their duty. We took control of our own destinies centuries ago when we cast off the gods, and embraced the notion of personal responsibility. We decided it was mankind that should be ultimately responsible for its actions, for its deeds, and once we did, our civilization advanced rapidly."

He looked at the reporters, every last one of them soon to be dead. "Yet today, through inaction, all that we built will be lost, but worse, so will the people who built it." He pointed at the building behind him. "Those men and women in there have forgotten that their responsibility is to the people of Atlantis, not the structures we have built. Atlantis is its people, not these streets, not these buildings. Yet soon, this will all be destroyed, and because of their inaction, so will you."

"What do you mean? Are you talking about the mountain?"

"Yes, I'm talking about the mountain. The earthquakes have been getting worse, not better as their scientists have been claiming, and the heat from the top of that beast"—he jabbed a finger at the mountain in the distance—"has been increasing at a terrifying rate. My team returned just yesterday from a two-week survey, and we have proof that the government has been lying to us. That mountain will soon explode, and if we don't take action, then we are all going to die."

"But what can we do? Is there any way to stop it?"

15

"No, not that our science knows of yet. Our only hope is evacuation."

Somebody guffawed. "How do you evacuate so many people? It's impossible!"

"Exactly. But we can save some, and some will be all we need to rebuild our great city when the calamity is over."

"And what if you're wrong?"

"Then I'm wrong, and you can all laugh at me in your reports, and I will be shunned for the rest of my life. But we will all be alive. Though if I'm right, and our city is indeed destroyed, then I will take no pleasure in saying 'I told you so,' because I too will be dead beside you. We must take action now and evacuate as many as we can, before it is too late. And this government, in its blind ignorance, refuses to act, too concerned to be thought the fool if I'm wrong.

"But I say we need to act now, get our people on the boats, and head east, back through the Pillars of Hercules, and find a safe location to settle until we see what happens to our home. And should I be wrong, those we sent will return. But if I am right, it will be those we were able to save who will rebuild Atlantis. And while it may not be here, on this island we call home, it will still be Atlantis, because Atlantis is its people, and it is its people that makes it great. Our knowledge, our ways, will allow us to rebuild, and perhaps even one day reclaim this home I fear will be lost any day now."

"Do you plan on running?"

He frowned at the reporter. "Running sounds like a coward's way out, and I am no coward. If I am permitted, I will leave with my family, and I pray that thousands will join me. But I fear, with my actions here today"—he held up the trident, giving it a shake—"I will be trapped inside a prison cell, condemned to die with the rest of you when the time comes." He sighed, lowering the trident to his side. "Now, I must go see my wife and children, before that ineffectual bunch behind me send their enforcers of ignorance to arrest me."

He pushed through the crowd, heading for the canal transport now pulling up to the dock serving the Senate, the members of the press chasing him, peppering him with questions. He climbed aboard, flashing his pass to the attendant, then took a seat, the press still onshore. The conductor reattached the boat to the water-powered line that stretched the length of the route along one of the many canals carved into the landscape, traveling from the sea to the edge of the mountain, three massive circular harbors surrounding the core of their civilization providing cross-access to the other parts of the city.

It was ingenious.

It was Atlantean.

And it would soon be lost to the world.

He closed his burning eyes, picturing his wife and young children dying in the massive explosion he knew was to come. His fist squeezed the trident tight as he decided he would not yield to fate. He had to save his family. He had to save as many as he could.

Yet he had no idea how.

Pico Island, Azores
Present Day

Command Sergeant Major Burt "Big Dog" Dawson stood staring out at the ocean, his eyes hunting for his friends. It had been almost half an hour since the earthquake, and though the damage appeared minor at the beach they had been enjoying, he had no clue what had happened underwater.

Sergeant Leon "Atlas" James jogged up, his massive frame glistening from the sun they had been enjoying. "No joy, BD. The dive shop said there's nothing we can do but wait. They had planned on a deep dive, so the fact we haven't seen them yet could be a good thing. If they panicked and tried to get to the surface quickly, they'd have the bends and could drown or die. He said it would take at least—"

Dawson cut him off as a sigh of relief escaped at the sight of their comrades in arms emerging from the water, Niner with a shit-eating grin, something gripped in his hand. The two slowly plodded toward them, their fins still on. Niner came to a stop in front of them and shoved the large...fork?...in the sand.

"I think I just discovered Atlantis."

Atlas eyed him. "I was looking for my fork. What are you doing with it?"

Niner tilted his head, giving him a look. "It's a trident, silly. Don't you know your comic books?"

Atlas took a deep breath, expanding his already massive frame. "I played with GI Joe when I was a kid."

"Yeah, well I'm Korean. Who do you think taught him the Kung Fu grip?"

Jimmy's eyes narrowed. "Umm, isn't Kung Fu Chinese?"

Niner shrugged. "What do I know? They make everything in China these days." He raised the trident from the ground then shoved it back in with a thud. "I am now the greatest archaeologist known to man." He looked about. "Where's my press?"

Dawson shook his head. "You two *do* know there was just an earthquake here."

Niner paused for a moment, his eyes surveying the area quickly before apparently deciding his inappropriate behavior could continue. "How do you think we found it? One minute it wasn't there, then a few minutes of rumbling, and voila, ancient city!"

Dawson paused for a moment as he processed what Niner was saying. "Wait a minute, you're actually serious, aren't you?"

Niner's eyes narrowed. "Umm, you *do* realize that this isn't a piece of the big man's kit, right? He *was* joking."

Dawson reached forward and rubbed at some of the sea that had made its life on the surface of the object, revealing what to him appeared to be gold. He grasped it and lifted. "Jeez, that's heavy."

"Exactly. Just like gold. And it's all mine."

Atlas grunted. "The government might have something to say about that. And if they don't, I still say it's my fork."

Dawson looked around them, the panic of earlier having settled down. "I think we should get this thing out of sight before it draws attention."

Niner hugged it, then gave it a little kiss. "Don't you worry, Forky, I won't let anyone take you from me."

Jimmy raised a tentative hand. "Umm, if I find a sock on the door to our room, can I bunk with one of you guys?"

Dawson and Atlas both answered in unison. "No!"

Dawson started heading for their vehicle. "You know who we should let know about this?"

Niner frowned. "Yeah, yeah, I know. Just give me a few minutes alone with it, though. I want to be able to say that for one brief moment in time, I was actually rich."

Acton/Palmer Residence
St. Paul, Maryland

Archaeology Professor James Acton lay on the floor of his bedroom, gasping for breath as his wife, Archaeology Professor Laura Palmer, lay beside him, one leg draped over the action, none the worse for wear. "Why am I the one who's so out of breath?"

She smiled at him and shrugged. "Sometimes it's nice to just lay back and enjoy the ride."

He chuckled then gave her a peck. "And did you?"

"Ooooh yeah!" She ran a finger over the scar on his shoulder, a reminder of his near-death experience in the West Bank. "Hurt?"

"Only if you touch it."

Her finger darted away, her jaw dropping. "Oh, God, I'm so sorry!"

He laughed. "Just kidding. No, it doesn't bother me at all. The Israeli surgeons did a great job." He rolled over to face her, their dirty bits coming back into contact. "I'm going to miss you."

She smiled at him. "I think you're going to miss *this*." She thrust her hips into him, causing a stirring below.

"Yup, I'm going to miss her too, but I think I'll miss the entire package."

She pushed him onto his back and straddled him. "Speaking of packages, how about this time I do all the work."

He grinned, clasping his hands behind his neck and staring up at the beauty that had agreed to marry him. "Sometimes it is nice to just lay back and enjoy the ride."

"Yeah, baby, you just lay there and let your wife do all the work."

Acton closed his eyes and groaned when his phone demanded his attention. He ignored it, instead giving himself over completely to the magic that was happening without him having to move a muscle. "I'm definitely going to miss you both." The phone buzzed again, then several more times, indicating a flurry of messages.

Laura pushed a hand into his chest. "Don't. You. Dare. Answer. That."

"Not a chance in hell."

The finish was furious, intense, and blinding—enough to fry his brain for a few minutes before his phone once again demanded attention. Laura, now draped across his chest, spent, suddenly pushed off him and stood, her legs straddling him, giving him a view his teenage self would have given his left testicle for.

"I'm done with you. You may now answer your phone."

He laughed and rolled to his feet as Laura headed for the bathroom. He grabbed his phone as the shower turned on, then dropped onto the bed, his eyes widening as he looked at the series of photos just sent to him. "Holy shit!" He saved them to the cloud then pulled them up on his iPad, using its bigger screen to scrutinize the photos of what Niner had discovered.

It appeared to be a trident, found after being underwater for quite some time, several close-ups showing exposed areas suggesting either pure gold or gold plating, but it was the final photo that had his heart hammering. "Hon, you've gotta see this!"

"Again? Wow, I guess you're really gonna miss me!"

He stared at the open door to their bathroom for a moment before he realized what she meant. "No, not Jim, Jr. Some photos Niner just sent us from the Azores."

"Give me a minute."

Acton stared at the image again, his excitement growing. "You're going to kick yourself if you don't get out here right now."

The shower turned off and he heard her step out, the sound of a towel pulled off the warming rack preceding damp feet padding toward him. She appeared in the doorway, soaked, with a towel around her torso, another in her hands, drying her hair.

"What is so important that I couldn't finish my shower?"

He flipped the iPad around, showing her the zoomed in portion of the image and her eyes widened. She hurried forward, reaching out for the iPad.

He jerked it away. "Nuh-uh, wet hands."

She frowned but dropped beside him on the bed, and he held it up again for her to see. "What is this?"

He swiped, showing her the photo of a grinning Niner holding the trident, which appeared taller than him, then a second with Atlas sitting at a table, a plate of food in front of him, pretending it was a fork.

"Where did they find it?"

"Diving off the Azores, according to the text. He thinks he found Atlantis."

Laura's eyes widened. "Wait a minute. Show me that first photo."

Acton flipped back to the zoomed in portion, showing an engraving that had him more excited than he could ever remember. She reached out and traced the three concentric rings without touching the screen.

"How did Plato describe it? A citadel at the center surrounded by three circular harbors?"

Acton nodded. "Exactly. With canals joining each of them. If this isn't an exact representation of what he described, I don't know what is."

Laura shook her head, finally tearing her eyes away from the screen. "But it can't be. Atlantis is just a myth."

Acton leaned away, holding his index fingers up and crossing them with a hiss. "Blasphemer!"

She gave him the eye. "Don't you dare start on me with Stargate. Between that, Star Wars, Star Trek, and Battlestar, it's a wonder I've stayed with you for as long as I have."

He put on his best pout.

She glared at him then lost it, unable to maintain the façade. She slapped his chest. "You can watch all the Stargate and whatever while I'm back in London for the next two weeks."

Acton held up the iPad. "I think we have to check this out."

"I think he's having you on."

Acton paused. "You don't think…" His eyes widened. "That bastard! You know what, he probably is!" He dialed the number and put the call on speaker, Niner's voice coming through loud and clear after the first ring.

"Hiya, Doc. You got my photos?"

"Yes, we did. You're on speaker with me and Laura."

"Hey sweetheart, still happy with that old man?"

Laura laughed. "Exquisitely!"

Niner groaned. "That's too bad. Oh well, I'll be waiting. So, what do you think?"

Acton held up the iPad. "Of your little joke?"

"Joke?"

"Yeah, joke. You're pulling my leg, right?"

"No, Doc, I'm not! Jimmy and I were scuba diving off the coast here when there was an earthquake. We were down a good ways, a couple of hundred feet, so we had to ride it out. When it was over and the dust settled, we found the ruins of a city. Big ass columns and collapsed buildings. It was incredible. Buried in the sand was this honkin' huge fork. I think it's a trident."

Acton chuckled. "It is."

Laura leaned closer to the phone. "And tell Atlas it could be priceless."

"So I should stop eating with it?"

They both laughed at Atlas' voice from the background.

"So what do you think? Am I not the greatest archaeologist in the world?"

Acton slowly shook his head. "Buddy, if this is what it could be, then your name could go down with the greats, like Carter, Leakey, and Woolley."

Niner groaned. "Man, I've never even heard of *one* of them. What's the point?"

Laura smiled. "You said you're in the Azores?"

"Yeah, can't say why or I'd have to kill your husband and marry you so you could be read in. Should I send this to you?"

They both vigorously shook their heads.

"No!" exclaimed Acton. "Just stay put. We're coming to you."

"When?"

"We'll be leaving as soon as we can. We'll text you the details."

"Okay, Docs, but make it snappy. We could be deployed at any minute."

"Understood. See you soon." Acton ended the call then leaped to his feet, heading for the closet where his luggage was kept, as Laura grabbed the phone and called their travel agent.

"Hi, Mary, it's me. We need a jet as soon as possible...yes, from here...Pico Island, Azores...ninety minutes?...we'll be there...yes, cancel my flight to London. Thanks."

And with that, his mega-millionaire wife had rebooked a private jet from her lease-share network. He was still getting used to the concept that his wife, and now both of them, were worth almost half a billion dollars. Her late brother had been an Internet tycoon years ago, and when he died tragically at one of her dig sites, he had left her his entire fortune gained by selling the company before the bubble had burst. They wanted for nothing, and tried to still keep things simple, though it did afford them certain luxuries like private jets.

"Oh, what about Hugh?"

Acton paused. "What about him?"

"Well, we were supposed to spend a couple of days together before my lectures. He took time off for it."

Acton thought for a moment. "Why not have him join us?"

She beamed at him. "That's a wonderful idea."

"And maybe have him bring his son. Wasn't he supposed to be on break from the police academy?"

"That's a fantastic idea! If this proves to be real, they'll be part of history."

Acton stood, staring at the photo still displayed on the iPad lying on the bed. "Do you think it is? I mean, do you think it could be?"

She turned away from the dresser then followed his gaze. "Assuming that prankster is telling us the truth, and there is some ancient city under the sea, offshore from the Azores, then it's definitely something. Some theories have suggested the Azores as a possible location for Atlantis, since it does lie past the Strait of Gibraltar and what some believe to be the Pillars of Hercules. Even if it isn't Atlantis, it could be a discovery of some significance." She motioned at the iPad. "And if that artifact is genuine, depending on when we can date it to, if it precedes Plato's description, it would be the first independent proof that the city once existed, even if the ruins Niner found aren't it."

Goosebumps traveled up and down Acton's body. "I feel like a schoolboy about to see his first set of—" He stopped himself.

Laura flashed him. "These?"

He grinned. "Time for one more?"

She wagged a finger at him. "Pack, Mister, or there'll be no Atlantis for you!"

Off the coast of Pico Island, Azores

Gavin Thatcher frowned as he pressed the button, the computer installed only recently on their boat immediately placing a scrambled call through a satellite orbiting far above them, the system then bouncing the signal around the globe, effectively making the call untraceable.

And it was technology he despised.

Technology, specifically communications technology, was responsible for the ills of the world today. Populations were split between left and right, with positions so entrenched, that they considered the other side evil and idiotic in any debate. Gone were the days of intelligent discourse, because anonymity over the cursed Internet allowed pile-on justice to prevail, with careers and dreams destroyed, businesses taken down, all by misinformed useful idiots hiding behind their smartphones.

Now there's *something that should never have been invented.*

And it extended beyond the borders of the modern states. Technology was allowing cultures to mix that simply weren't compatible. Gone were the days when someone left their homeland for a better life, then integrated and became part of the melting pot that was their new home. Now, with technology, one never had to say goodbye to family or friends in the old country, could listen to the same radio stations, watch the same television shows, and read the same newspapers, without even bothering to learn the language of your new home. And then when asked to integrate, those same useful idiots would pile on and claim those asking were racists for doing so.

All because of technology.

It was destroying the world. Some might call him a Luddite, but he didn't shun all technology. Much of it was passive and contributed to the betterment of mankind, like medical technology. It was communications technology that was the true evil, but until recently, there was little his band of true believers could have done about it.

But several months ago, when he had met the man he was waiting to be connected to, for the first time in his life he truly had hope. What they were preparing to do wouldn't change the world, not today, but it might make people realize just how dependent they had become on modern communications technology, and just how vulnerable it was to attack. It was their hope this would stimulate conversations among those so dependent upon the Internet, that perhaps they might come out from behind their screens and actually talk to their neighbor about something, rather than rant to the like-minded on the social media sites

30

they frequented, social media sites that filtered the news and posts they saw to only match their beliefs.

It would be a long, hard fight, but before the day was out, the beginning of the end could well be underway.

The system beeped and a silhouetted figure appeared, the voice and image of their benefactor never having been revealed to anyone else since their initial meeting. It made him nervous, though it didn't matter. His pockets were deep, and because of him, they were almost there.

"Thatcher. You have an update?"

"Yes, sir, and I'm afraid it's bad news. We've had an earthquake here and it buried the device. We're digging it out now, but it could take hours, maybe even until tomorrow."

There was a pause, and if a silhouette could look displeased, this one did. "That's unfortunate. If this is to succeed, we need total coverage."

"Yes, sir."

"Contact me as soon as you're finished."

"Yes, sir."

The system went dark and he sighed, his heart pounding like it always did when dealing with the man. He didn't trust him, but trust wasn't necessarily required. His money had been there when needed, and as far as he knew, every single device was in place along the entire European seaboard except for one, and he was responsible. Though that would be resolved shortly.

Then a message would be sent the world couldn't ignore.

MessageStream Office #42

Atlantis

Before the fall

Mestor stood at the communications center, impatiently waiting for an update. As the messages arrived from around the city through the high-pressure water pipe delivery system, each waterproof container was opened by one of the operators, the destination examined, then redirected if necessary, handed to a runner if it was to be personally delivered, or announced publicly then placed on file for pick up. It was a fantastic system that allowed messages to be delivered quickly and efficiently throughout the city, and it was why he now stood here, waiting for an update on the situation that was developing at the Senate. Professor Ampheres had spoken, some of his group present, and a message had been dispatched, telling him to be ready to act.

"Message for Mestor!"

His heart pounded and he raised a hand, stepping toward the dispatcher. "I'm Mestor."

"Identification."

He showed him his ID, and the tied scroll containing his message was handed to him. He quickly stepped away from the crowd, unrolling the page, his eyes widening at the report.

Unbelievable!

Ampheres had said everything they had expected him to, and he had been ignored, exactly as expected. But then he had done something foolish.

Stealing the trident? Is he insane?

It made him a target. Denouncing the government was legal. They couldn't touch him for his words. But stealing the trident? That would have him arrested for sure, and an arrested man was not only easy to silence in the short term, he was easy to discredit in the long. It had been an idiotic, impulsive action. But what was done, was done, and they had to act quickly if they were to protect him.

He stepped up to the message stand, grabbing several forms, quickly scribbling his messages, then rolling them up and tying them off, making certain the final destination was visible. He handed them over to the dispatcher, then the coins to pay for the express service. He waited to see the messages loaded into the tubes, then the access port on each appropriate pipe opened and the tubes dropped inside, the flowing water whipping them toward their destination. He nodded at the clerk then headed for the dock Ampheres would soon be arriving at. He just prayed that the government hadn't already sent word to have the Enforcers waiting for the foolish scientist.

Otherwise, there could be blood.

Pico Airport

Pico Island, Azores

Present Day

Professor James Acton grinned and waved at the group of men waiting for them on the tarmac. Not too long ago, these same men had killed his students, and tried to kill him, all based upon false intel provided by a corrupt administration, indicating he was the head of a domestic terror cell, and his students were his followers who had already killed US personnel associated with DARPA. This Delta team, members of 1st Special Forces Operational Detachment-Delta, had eliminated what they thought was a terror cell, and once they discovered the truth, refused to follow their illegal orders, nearly resulting in the death of the man now approaching them with his hand extended, Command Sergeant Major Burt "Big Dog" Dawson. Acton shook his hand while Laura was embraced by her biggest fans, Niner and Atlas. After years of atonement, these men were now friends, their past sins forgiven, the sight of them no longer causing fear.

"Great to see you guys," said Acton as he shook the others' hands. He gestured at their surroundings. "Kind of an odd place for you guys to be, isn't it?"

Dawson led them toward a nearby vehicle. "No, Lajes Air Base is here, and it's quite often used as a layover point. We're between missions and the Colonel gave us a few days on the beaches."

Acton couldn't keep up with the pleasantries anymore. "Which is when you guys found the trident?"

Niner held up a finger. "Umm, *I* found it. If there's any reward, it goes to me. I've got family starving back in Korea to feed."

Atlas slugged Niner's shoulder, sending him stumbling to the side. "Your parents are from *South* Korea. I thought we settled this."

Niner shrugged. "Jimmy met them. You saw how skinny they were."

Jimmy gave him a look. "No skinnier than you, you tool. Ever heard of genetics?"

Acton grinned at Laura, always loving the banter between the various Bravo Team members, their bond so tight, even the most outrageous insults were always taken in good fun.

He loved it.

Dawson opened the rear of an SUV, then looked about to see if anyone was watching. Niner darted ahead, presenting a blanket wrapped object with the aplomb of a grand marshal in a royal court.

"M'Lady, M'Lord, I present to you, the Fork of Atlantis."

"Fork of Atlas!" coughed the big man.

Niner gave Atlas the eye, then flipped the blanket aside. Acton gasped as his heart pounded, there still some doubt until this moment as to whether they were being set up for a prank. He immediately began taking video with his phone as Laura climbed in the back, a measuring tape out.

"The object is one-hundred-eight-two centimeters long from end to end, thirty-four centimeters at its widest point, and sixteen centimeters in circumference around the base." She lifted it gently. "The object is heavy, implying either solid metal, or metal plating over metal or stone. The exposed areas, here and here"—she indicated several locations scraped clear of the barnacles encrusting the object—"suggest at a minimum gold plating, though my initial guess is that it is solid gold from the weight. When we properly weigh it, we'll know." She pointed at the engraving that had them so excited back home. "This engraving seems to match the description Plato gave of Atlantis—"

"So I did discover Atlantis?" interrupted an obviously elated Niner. He shoved Jimmy. "I *told* you!"

"—*suggests* that it could be from Atlantis, thus proving it wasn't a myth, or it could merely be an artifact created after Plato wrote his description in *Timaeus*. We won't know until we can carbon date the surface buildup."

Dawson leaned forward. "Can you carbon date the gold itself?"

Acton shook his head. "No, in order to carbon date something, it has to have carbon in it. Gold is a base element, so it can't contain carbon. The barnacles that have built up on this over the years should allow us to figure out how long it has been underwater, since they contain carbon. If that predates Plato's writings, then it would strongly suggest that either Atlantis did exist, or Plato was inspired by some other city for his story."

Atlas leaned against the SUV, the suspension protesting. "This Plato dude, why's he so important? Beyond inventing playdough and being some ancient Greek philosopher, why is he so tied to Atlantis?"

Laura climbed back out of the SUV. "Because the first known reference to Atlantis was contained in his book, where it described an advanced civilization that lay beyond the Pillars of Hercules, with an incredible city built in concentric circles, with harbors and canals carved into the island, in ever greater widths." She pointed at the engraving. "Exactly like that."

Dawson scratched the stubble on his chin. "Were there any other writings?"

"Yes, after his, there were others, but all seemed to be referring back to his initial text, then trying to attribute other things in history to the Atlanteans, that had previously been thought to be other cultures. Really, so few texts still exist from back then, there's no real way to know. Most modern academics believe that Atlantis was merely a metaphor that Plato used to describe the perfect civilization that he felt Greece should strive toward, and in fact, the Atlanteans were the bad guys in his narrative."

Niner grunted. "Bad Atlanteans? That fits what my Stargate tells me." He folded his arms. "Well, there's another way to settle this."

Acton smiled at him. "Pay a visit to where you found it."

38

Off the coast of Pico Island, Azores

Acton was giddy and impatient as they slowly descended toward what could be the greatest discovery not only of his career, but in the history of modern man. This would likely rival, if not put to shame, Carter's discovery of King Tut's tomb nearly a century ago.

And for that reason, he had to control himself. While he now had no doubt Niner and Jimmy had indeed found something—there was no way this was a practical joke—it was likely just an ancient city, long lost to the sea, and *not* the fabled city of Atlantis. He had to not get his hopes up, and he also had to remain calm, controlling his breathing as well as rate of descent, scuba diving something he had done on several occasions, but was in no way expert at.

Fortunately, Laura's travel agent had arranged state of the art equipment for them, and Niner and Dawson were sporting the gear that awaited Reading and his son's arrival. All four of them had masks that allowed them to talk to one another, though that left Jimmy and Atlas out of the conversation, much to Niner's delight.

"We should be getting close." Niner pointed ahead. "I'm pretty sure this is where the landslide happened."

Dawson glanced at him. "*Pretty* sure?"

"Hey, it's not like I had a GPS down here, but after we found the fork, we went straight up, and you guys were directly ahead of us onshore, so we couldn't have drifted that far either way."

Atlas turned, waving at them, then pointed ahead, a blue shark swimming by, paying them no mind.

"I think the big guy just spotted something to eat," said Niner. "We should have brought the fork."

Acton peered into the murkiness, in the direction Atlas was pointing, when he gasped. "Forget the king-size Filet-O-Fish, I think he's pointing at that." He leaned forward, kicking hard toward what appeared to be a set of columns sticking up from the seabed, the others following, their lights all directed toward what Atlas had spotted.

"My word!" gasped Laura. "Part of me still thought you were pulling our leg, Niner, but..." Her voice trailed off in awe, and Acton for a moment was lost in the excitement as his pulse pounded in his ears. He finally remembered he was a scientist, and grabbed the camera floating around his neck, activating it.

"Let's remember, this whole area could be unstable, so stay off the seabed if you can, and try not to touch anything."

"Yeah, especially you, meatball," added Niner. "Ah, shit, he can't hear me. Somebody remind me to insult him when we go topside."

Acton turned to face Atlas and Jimmy, pointing at the seabed and waving his hands and shaking his head, then doing the same with the ruins around them. Both gave him a thumbs up, and they proceeded deeper into the revealed portion of what was clearly an ancient city, the architecture suggesting Ancient Greek, though with significant differences. There was also the fact that the Greeks had never traveled this far, at least according to currently understood history.

But there was no denying that an ancient, advanced civilization had once thrived here, the size of the exposed city significant, and suggesting the center of a metropolis, as opposed to a few scattered homes. Small villages didn't build large buildings supported by towering columns. And island based indigenous cultures didn't either. This was clearly built by some ancient European based culture, either previously unknown, or previously unknown to have traveled this far into the Atlantic.

"So, Docs, is it Atlantis?"

Acton glanced over at Niner, about ten feet to his left. "Too soon to tell, but it definitely appears to be from the right era, with the proper influences you'd expect from a culture that would have developed from a Mediterranean one." He glanced over at Laura. "Let's place the geolocators so we can easily find it again."

"Okay." Laura retrieved two devices from her bag, activating one and dropping it to the seabed, then swimming a short distance and releasing the backup device.

"It's getting pretty late, so I think we should head to the surface. We'll come back tomorrow and make a real go of it."

41

Niner groaned like a child. "Awww, do we have to?"

Acton chuckled. "We'll have all day tomorrow, and we'll come back with more equipment so we can take a proper survey. Trust me, tomorrow is when the fun begins."

They began their slow ascent, Acton reviewing the footage on the camera's display, barely seeing anything, but too excited to patiently wait for later. When he finally broke the surface, their guide waved to him, and he swam over to the rented boat.

"Did you find anything good?"

Acton climbed in and shook his head, giving the others a look as they joined him. "No, nothing. We'll come back tomorrow and keep looking, it's all good fun just the same."

"It is that." Their guide fired up the engine, slowly taking them back to shore, everyone remaining silent as they stripped from their gear. Acton wasn't a fan of lying, but he couldn't risk having their guide know they had found something of significance, then tell his friends. There'd be dozens of boats and scores of divers by dawn. In fact, tomorrow, he'd pay extra to take the boat out themselves, and leave the guide behind.

Dawson's phone vibrated and he took the call, stepping toward the back of the boat as it pulled up to the dock. They disembarked and he rejoined them. "I'm afraid you'll be on your own tomorrow."

Laura looked at him. "Why's that?"

"We've been put on standby."

Acton frowned. "That's too bad, but I guess duty calls. We'll keep you posted on what we find."

Niner jabbed a finger at him as they climbed into their SUV. "You better. I want my cut."

Acton laughed. "Buddy, the only way you're making any money off this is if you sell the film rights."

Niner stared at the roof of the SUV wistfully. "And then maybe I can star in it too!"

Atlas groaned. "Oh, man, let's not have that discussion again. Soldiers shouldn't play themselves in movies."

Dawson glanced in the rearview mirror as they pulled away, Niner holding his hands in front of him, mimicking a camera lens. Dawson gave Acton a look. "Why oh why did you plant that idea in his head?"

"All right Mr. DeMille, I'm ready for my close-up!"

Acton shook his head at Niner. "I think maybe it's a good thing you guys are leaving. He's going to be unbearable, and at least you guys are armed."

Atlantean Enforcer's Office, Western District

Atlantis

Before the fall

Senior Enforcer Kleito sat in her office, reading over a report about damage to the Museum of the Gods suffered in last night's earthquake. She knew from her dispatches that the news reporters only had half the story, if that. Their orders, handed down from the Secretary of Public Order, was to cordon off any damage, keeping eyewitnesses to a minimum. City maintenance crews would arrive within minutes, teams on standby throughout the city, and the mess would be cleaned up, then repairs made as quickly as possible, usually under the guise of planned work, as stone-based architecture took time to fix.

The population was being kept in the dark, and she didn't agree with that decision by their duly elected representatives. But she dared not question it. She had just received her promotion, and she wasn't about to put her career at risk questioning what she had to assume was a decision made for reasons simply unknown to her. While the smoking mountain that dominated the skyline concerned her, she was certain there was no danger, otherwise the government would have taken action by now.

The fringe elements were, of course, out in full force, claiming pending doom, but they had always existed, long before the earthquakes began. Killer waves, angry gods, invasion fleets from beyond the Pillars of Hercules, even massive rocks from the skies, were always dominating the conversations of those with too much time on their hands.

There was a knock on her door and she glanced up to see her assistant standing there, a concerned look on his face. "What is it?"

He stepped forward, handing her a message. "Urgent message from the Senate."

Her eyebrows rose slightly as she unrolled it, then jumped when she read it, recognizing the name of one of the city's most prominent intellectuals. "We're to arrest Professor Ampheres? We're sure this is legit?"

He shrugged. "I could request confirmation."

She shook her head, rising from her chair. "No, that would take too long. Let's assume it is, and sort it out later." She marched through the door and pointed at four officers. "You're with me." They all leaped to their feet and followed her outside as she broke into a jog, heading for the docks where one of the most respected scientists of the city was due to arrive.

With orders to arrest him for the theft of Poseidon's Trident.

Off the coast of Pico Island, Azores

Present Day

James Acton checked his gauge, confirming he still had plenty of time to enjoy himself almost 200 feet below the surface. When he and Laura had arrived this morning, there was no evidence that anyone had discovered their find, and the owner of the diving supplies company had no problem taking an extra hundred to leave the guide behind. Their boat was far overhead, most of their equipment it had ferried from shore now on the ocean floor. All it now contained were additional tanks and the trident, carefully wrapped and stowed, they having decided this morning that leaving it at the hotel might be riskier than taking it with them. Hugh Reading and his son Spencer were due to arrive later today, and they'd then have their own built-in security detail.

He checked the waterproof tablet computer hung around his neck, swiping his finger to the left several times, confirming all the camera feeds were working, all but one showing a crystal clear image. "Camera Six seems to be down."

Laura, to his left, kicked toward the position. "Give me a sec." She disappeared behind some ruins, then a few moments later the image flickered, giving a clear view of her grinning face.

"Can you see me now?"

"Either you or a mermaid."

"Hey, if this turns out to be Atlantis, maybe they're real too."

"Better not mention that to Hugh, he'll call you daft or barmy or some other Briticism. Or is that Britishism?"

Laura reappeared from behind a still intact wall. "Who knows when you're making up words?" She motioned around them. "We now have complete coverage of the area. I think we're ready to deploy the relay."

"Yes'm." Acton swam down to one of their bags lying on the seafloor and unzipped it. He pulled out a weighted device, activated it, and after following the prompts on the screen, it was soon connecting to the signals of all eight cameras now deployed on the seabed. "We've got a good connection. Deploying now."

He placed the heavy relay on the seafloor, then unhooked the end of the flexible antenna from the circular weight. He let it go and the buoyant end slowly rose toward the surface, the light cable uncoiling from within the bag. He carefully helped feed it through so there weren't any snags, and within minutes, the display updated, indicating it had connected with the satellite providing their link to the cloud storage that would record all of their footage. If anyone tried to disturb the site, or if, God forbid, there was another landslide that might send what had been revealed farther down the side of what was a massive volcano originating on the bottom of the Atlantic, they'd have video of everything that had occurred, and perhaps proof of what they hoped these ruins might represent. "We're connected."

"Excellent! Ready to explore?"

He smiled at his wife, about thirty feet away. "Let's. This place will be getting a whole lot more crowded once we put out the word tonight."

"I do feel a little guilty about not notifying anyone yet, but, well…"

Acton chuckled. "I know. Sometimes it's fun to be a little selfish. Besides, I'll feel better once Hugh and Spencer are here."

"Me too."

Acton struck a near-weightless superhero pose. "What? I'm not man enough for you?"

Laura looked back at him and laughed. "My hero!"

"Damn skippy, and you best not forget it!"

"Okay, hero, let's get to work. I'm going to start mapping the south side, closest to the island. You start on the north."

Acton became all business. "Roger that. Watch your gauges. We'll have to surface in a little bit to swap tanks, and the ascent takes almost thirty minutes."

"Okay."

Acton pushed back a few feet from the relay device now sending signals halfway across the world, and examined the area. Scattered across the surface were columns and collapsed walls, and what appeared to be cobblestone roads and walkways, long since split apart and scattered. He worked his way deeper, taking pictures and video with his camera, taking notes on his tablet, and was soon lost in the thrill of a new discovery. An alarm beeped and it startled him before he realized what it was—the timer warning him he was due to surface.

He checked his indicator and frowned at the reading showing slightly less pressure than he was expecting, his excitement causing him to breathe heavier than usual. "I have to surface. How's your pressure gauge reading?" He looked back toward the ruins for Laura, but couldn't make them out.

You must have traveled farther than you realized.

"I'm good, but I'll surface with you."

"Okay, I'll start coming back toward you." He turned back away from where he thought the ruins were, and marked his coordinates on the tablet so he could continue from the same spot.

And paused.

"What's that?"

"What's what?"

His eyes narrowed as he peered into the distance, trying to pick out what he had seen, but failing. He reached up and flicked off his suit's lights, the entire area abruptly an inky black except for the glow from his tablet, which he pressed against his stomach, smothering its light.

"Hon, are you okay?"

He squinted, then slowly swam toward whatever it was he was seeing.

"Hon?"

He recognized the concern in Laura's voice. "Sorry, I think I see something."

"What?"

"I'm not sure. I think it's a light, but it can't be. It must be something highly reflective."

"That doesn't make sense. Even if it was a mirror, it would still need a light source to reflect."

Acton had to agree, but there was no denying what he was now seeing. Directly ahead, there was a light source that grew clearer the closer he got. "It's definitely a light."

"Could it be a volcanic vent?"

"Jeez, I hope not, but with the earthquake, who knows."

"What color is it?"

Acton smiled at the astute question. "Not red or orange. It's white. Very white. Artificial white."

"Could someone else be down here with us?"

Acton's heart rate picked up a few points at the thought. They hadn't had much of a chance to survey the area, instead focusing on the initial find made by Niner. For all they knew, there could be a massive site farther down the mountain, and someone else could be there, looting it.

He kicked harder, and the light not only became clearer, but silhouettes began to form. "There's definitely someone else down here."

"Be careful. You don't know who they are. They could be dangerous."

Acton slowed, then held up his camera, zooming in for a better view. He took a picture, hoping to focus in on the resulting image, and cursed when the forgotten flash lit up the area.

All the silhouettes stopped what they were doing and turned toward him.

Oh shit!

"They've seen me."

"Get back here! We'll sort it out up top."

The figures were now swimming toward him.

"They're coming my way." He kicked toward the surface, hard, then slowed, remembering he'd get the bends if he ascended too quickly.

"I'm coming to you."

Acton shook his head uselessly. "No! If they're hostile, they don't know about you. Go topside. Don't forget to watch your rate of ascent. When you get there, call Hugh and let him know what's going on, just in case. Call Greg too."

"Are you sure?"

"Absolutely. If these guys mean us any harm, one of us needs to let somebody know what's going on."

"Okay, be careful."

The fear in her voice was palpable, and he cursed their lives of the past few years, where everything that could go wrong, did. If it weren't for their previous bad experiences, it might not have even occurred to him that these people could be bad. Yet paranoia had saved their lives too many times, and if these people were so innocent, why were they rapidly approaching him? Why not just send one person for an underwater greeting?

No, something was wrong.

One of the figures, still silhouetted from the light behind them, reached out and grabbed one of his companions, and their pursuit slowed. He smiled.

That's right, you guys can't surface too quickly either.

He had at least fifty feet of depth on them, so should reach the surface first, and Laura was even farther ahead than him, exploring the shallower side of the find. She would reach the boat first. "When you get topside, take the boat to the shore where there are people."

"What about you?"

"I'll swim."

"Bollocks!"

"I want you safe, where there are people, and can get help."

He heard a deep sigh over the comm. "Fine. What's happening?"

Acton stared at his pursuers as he continued to gently kick toward the surface. "They've slowed. I guess they don't want the bends either."

"Then you should have time."

"I should, but I still want you to go to—" He heard something behind him and he spun as he was suddenly overwhelmed by an intensely bright light. He raised his hand to shield his eyes, squinting as his ears made sense of what they were hearing. "Shit, they've got some sort of submersible! It's right in front of me!"

"James, are you okay?"

"I'm okay, but it's like five feet from me. There's no way I can get away!"

"What do they want? Oh God, what's happening?"

Acton waved at the vehicle, the size of a small car, a set of robotic arms visible, extending toward him. "They're trying to grab me!" He spun around and kicked hard, away from the submersible, but he could hear its motors kick in, the sound getting louder as it neared. He looked up at the surface, still too far above, debating if the bends were worth it, but realized it didn't matter—he couldn't outrun a machine.

He stopped and slowly turned around, waving his surrender at the submersible, then pointing toward the surface. The arms retracted, and the machine backed off a few feet, the message apparently received.

"I'm surrendering to them and they backed off. You get to the surface and go for help."

"O-okay, you be careful. Watch your ascent."

"I will. I love you."

Laura gasped out a cry, her voice cracking. "I-I love you too. I'm almost there. I'll call Greg first, just in case I can't reach Hugh. He might be in the air."

"That-that sounds good."

"Okay, I can see the boat. I'm almost...wait, something's wrong."

"What?"

"Oh my God. No! Let me go! Let me—!"

There was a burst of static when the comm suddenly went silent.

"Laura! Laura! What's happening? Laura!"

Off the coast of Pico Island, Azores

Gavin Thatcher stared at their two prisoners, both zip-tied and blindfolded, and shook his head. He closed the door and stepped back out onto the deck, the men who had captured them standing at the bow. "Why the hell did you take them?"

One of the men, Tark Gerald, shrugged. "He saw what we were doing."

"So? He saw some men working on an undersea cable. How would he know what we were actually doing? All you had to do was wave him off, but instead, you chased him in a submersible and attacked the woman he was diving with!" He threw his hands up in the air in frustration. "Now we have two prisoners who know we're up to something. What the hell do we do now?"

Another shrug. "Kill them?"

Thatcher spun at him, his eyes and mouth wide with horror. "Are you kidding me? We're not killers! What the hell do you think we're trying to do here? We're trying to save lives by making the world realize it's too dependent upon modern technology! We're trying to force people to interact more, to learn from each other, to empathize with each other, by reintroducing them to good old-fashioned face-to-face conversations. This entire exercise is to prevent the violence that is resulting from a lack of human contact. And you propose to further that cause by killing two of the people we're actually trying to save?"

Tark stared at the deck. "Sorry, I just thought it was more important to, you know, save the mission. Better to lose two than the thousands or millions to come."

Thatcher stared at him for a moment. The idiot was right, in a simplistic fashion. It was why they had weapons. And if these two people had indeed been a threat, he could understand the logic, though still wouldn't have condoned their deaths. But they had never been a threat. One had stumbled upon something he didn't understand, and the team had overreacted. "Okay, well they can't stay here. We've got work to do, and I don't want to risk having them on board, just in case one of them gets loose or someone comes looking for them." He pointed at Tark and one of his buddies, Oswald "Spud" Fletcher. "You two take them ashore and secure them until we're done."

"Where?"

Thatcher growled with frustration. "Do I need to think of everything? Just take them somewhere they won't be found!"

"And should they try to escape?"

Thatcher clasped his hands behind his neck, closing his eyes. "Don't let them."

"But if they should?"

Thatcher sighed, dismayed by what he was about to say. "Then kill them. We can't risk the mission being compromised."

Pico Island, Azores

Acton glared at the two men holding them, their guns tucked into their belts the only thing stopping him from attacking. In a fair fight, he was pretty sure he could take them both, especially if Laura were helping. They had been trained extensively over the past several years by Laura's ex-SAS security team, all former members of the British Special Air Services, their equivalent to Special Forces. And, Acton was willing to bet he and Laura had seen more actual combat than these two.

But they had guns, and he couldn't risk a stray bullet taking them out, at least not yet.

"What hotel are you staying at?"

Acton didn't reply.

The man tapped his gun. "I'll put a bullet in your lady friend if you'd like."

Acton stared at him. "If you lay a finger on her, you're dead."

The man laughed. "Tough talk." He tapped the gun. "Where?"

"Aldeia das Adegas."

"Is anyone expecting you?"

Acton shook his head, deciding the better play was to leave out the fact Reading and his son were due to arrive soon.

"When are you due to leave?"

"Tomorrow."

"How?"

"By air."

"What flight?"

Acton hesitated. "I'm not sure."

"What airline?"

"Umm, United."

The man stared at him suspiciously for a moment, then pulled out his phone, tapping at the display. "Bullshit. United doesn't fly here." He leaned closer, tempting Acton's foot to embed itself in the man's groin. "What flight?"

"We have a private jet."

Acton's eyes darted toward Laura, wondering why she would tell them that. Then he suppressed a smile. Greed was an overwhelming force, and if they could use her—their—money to their advantage, they might just get these men to screw up, or buy their freedom.

Both men's eyebrows rose, a quick glance exchanged.

"Private jet? What are you, rich?"

Laura nodded. "Impossibly."

Way to go, babe, pour it on!

"And we can make it worth your while to let us go."

There was little doubt there was an internal debate going on in the lead captor's mind, and Acton had to admit he was not only surprised, but dismayed at what came out of the man's mouth.

"So this jet, it can leave whenever you want?"

"Yes."

"Good. Then that's what we'll do. We'll take your jet off the island, then we won't have to worry about anyone finding us."

Public Transport Station #6, Western Sector

Atlantis

Before the fall

Ampheres stepped off the canal transport and moved with the crowd toward the street above. A commotion just above eye level from the steps had him gripping the upside-down trident tighter, and adjusting his robe now covering the top of the relic tucked under his clothing, if only partially. Feet pounding on stone, in unison, confirmed his greatest fears.

Enforcers.

And he had little doubt they were here for him. Crime was rare in Atlantis, as want was even rarer. There was no need to steal here, though that didn't mean crimes of passion didn't still occur. And it sometimes meant bored Enforcers were a little overzealous when they were called upon.

He spotted them at the edge of the square in front of the docks, and he froze. There was no escaping them, as he had nowhere to go. The only reason they were here and not at his home waiting for him, was probably because they had received word through the MessageStream that he would be arriving now, like the fool he was.

Why not get off at the stop before?

Or after?

Because you have no experience being a fugitive from the law!

His shoulders slumped in defeat, there little point in resisting.

Somebody gripped his left arm and he nearly soiled himself.

"Professor Ampheres, do exactly as I say, and you *will* get out of this."

He stared at the man now beside him. "Wh-who are you?"

"My name is Mestor, and I'm a friend. That's all you need to know for now. Come with me."

Mestor pulled on his arm, and rather than resist, Ampheres let himself be led at a brisk but inconspicuous pace, perpendicular to the arriving Enforcers. They stopped behind an obelisk honoring the founding fathers and mothers, and the man released his grip. He pulled a nondescript hooded robe from his bag and tossed it over Ampheres' shoulders.

"Give me that." Mestor reached out for the trident and Ampheres reluctantly handed it to him. "Now fix yourself." Mestor stuffed the head of the trident into the bag, covering the exposed end with a large cloth, hiding most of the precious relic as Ampheres fixed his new robe in place. Mestor pointed to the far end of the square.

62

"Now, go to the street, then turn right, away from your home. I will join you in a few minutes."

Ampheres eyed the trident. "I should take that."

Mestor shook his head. "No, they're looking for a man that fits your description, carrying this. Your hands are now empty, and you've changed your clothes, something they won't be anticipating. Now go, before it's too late!"

Ampheres nodded, then stepped out from behind the obelisk, resisting the urge to check over his shoulder and see what the Enforcers were doing. He could hear shouts of annoyed citizens not used to the law's interference in their daily lives, and it terrified him. He quickened his pace as his heart hammered, then caught himself just as he was about to break out into a jog.

Calm yourself!

He slowed, drawing a deep breath, then exhaled slowly, repeating the process until he neared the street. He almost went left toward his home and his family, before he remembered his instructions and broke right. He walked along the pedestrian mall, quaint shops lining the canal, hawking wares to the traveling public, too many food stalls to count offering to save time with deliciously prepared meals. The lunch crowd was just arriving, the street thickening with those who toiled inside rather than in the fields surrounding the mountain.

The ground rumbled, shrieks erupting around him as he struggled to keep his balance, but it lasted only a few heartbeats, nervous laughter quickly replacing the momentary panic, and those around him continued on as if nothing had happened. He glanced over his shoulder at the mountain, still steaming, still warning an ignorant population of what was to come.

But only if you're right.

He was sure he was, yet how could he be? His team had little science to work with. The entire concept of an erupting mountain was foreign to them, as their entire civilization had lived on this massive island for countless centuries, and never in their entire recorded history had there been any evidence that this was nothing beyond a regular mountain like any other they knew existed in the lands to the east.

There were reports of erupting mountains from the stories brought back by their scouts, yet none had ever seen the events described, and until the mountain here had begun to send puffs of steam into the sky, it had never occurred to anyone that this was one of those.

But what did that mean? The stories suggested destruction was possible on an unimaginable scale, but were they just stories? His own from his youth grew in exaggeration with each telling. The meal got slightly bigger each time, the bottles of wine drunk ever increasing. Were these stories any different?

"The end is near! Repent and beg Poseidon for forgiveness!"

The rants of the raging man snapped him out of his reverie, the crowd giving the man a wide berth, and Ampheres wondered if he had always been this way, or had he been triggered like he had the moment the mountain had awoken.

What would happen if the government announced the possible impending destruction?

He frowned as he passed the man. Would there be panic in the streets? Would this poor soul be multiplied a thousand-fold as his fellow Atlanteans resigned themselves to their fate? Or would they unite and solve the problem, as they had so many times before throughout their history?

He feared it would be a mix of both, as there wasn't a solution to save everyone. The only way for that was to evacuate the island, and there weren't enough boats, and even if there was time to build enough, there wasn't enough wood. That resource was relatively scarce. Centuries ago, forestry management had been introduced, vast plantations now providing them with a sustainable supply, but only to maintain their basic requirements, not to build fleets of boats to sail tens of thousands of people to distant lands.

No, no matter what happened, the majority would die should he be proven right. The best Atlantis could hope for was that enough would survive to rebuild their civilization somewhere else.

Someone gripped his arm and he nearly fainted before he realized it was his savior.

"Come, there's little time."

"What about my family?"

"If everything has gone to plan, they are already safe."

"Who are you?"

"A friend."

Ampheres stopped. "That's not good enough."

Mestor cursed. "Fine, but at least walk with me while I explain. We can't risk being caught."

Ampheres agreed that was probably wise, and resumed their brisk pace.

"My name is Mestor. I'm a graduate student from the Poseidon Institute. We came to the same conclusion you did last week, and presented our findings to the government, and like you, our findings were ignored. Unlike you, none of us stole Poseidon's damned Trident!"

Ampheres frowned. "It was rather stupid, wasn't it?"

"It was, and it also pretty much discredited you completely. Now, any press reports about you will be that you are a whack-job who stole a priceless relic after spouting nonsense, and that discredits us all. In one foolish stroke, you've essentially wiped out any hope we have of warning the population."

Ampheres' chest ached with Mestor's words, for they were probably right. He had conducted himself with dignity, enough that some in the Senate might have begun to question the official government line, but as soon as he had let anger rule him, he had lost all credibility. He had little doubt that his words were not spoken of from that moment on, but only his actions. It was a completely wasted opportunity, and it had probably cost the lives of every single Atlantean.

He looked at Mestor. "Why are you here?"

Mestor guided him down an alleyway. "I was to meet you after your speech, in the hopes you would join our cause. This afternoon, when the workers are heading home, we were to stage a protest in front of the Senate, demanding action, and handing out information on what is going on, to try and wake up the sheep that surround us. But now that your speech will be linked with us, I fear it will fall on deaf ears."

"Then why not leave me to the Enforcers?"

"Because Professor Gadeiros told me to protect you."

Ampheres nearly came to a halt, but Mestor grabbed him by the arm and urged him forward. "Professor Gadeiros? He was my mentor in university! I haven't seen him in ages."

"Yes, apparently you were a great disappointment to him."

Ampheres frowned. "He told you about that?"

"He told me what happened."

"That's unfortunate. I don't come off too well in that story."

Mestor regarded him. "No, you don't. Why he wants to save you and your family is beyond me, after what you did."

Ampheres' eyes burned. "I was in love, and young."

They emerged onto another street, less busy, and Mestor had them heading to the left, deeper into a residential area of the great city.

"My understanding is you were in love with two women."

Ampheres shook his head, the memories flooding back, the shame and hurt of it all something he hadn't thought about in years. "Mestor, I'll give you a free piece of advice."

Mestor's eyebrows rose. "What?"

"Never fall in love with your mentor's daughter, then fall for her friend. It can never end well."

Mestor grunted. "Trust me, I'm not that stupid."

Ampheres laughed. "I was considered one of the brightest to ever come out of the university, yet I still messed things up. The heart and

67

mind are two different things, and unfortunately, you can only educate one of them. I broke a woman's heart that I loved, I lost my mentor, and the path I thought had been laid out for me. Fortunately, Professor Gadeiros was a better man than me, and didn't destroy my reputation as he could have. Instead, he merely cut me out of his life."

Mestor pointed to a building to their right and they made a beeline for it. "Was it worth it?"

Ampheres nodded. "In the long run, absolutely. My wife was the other woman, and I now have three children. I followed a new path that has been rewarding." The ground rumbled for a brief second and they both paused. "Unfortunately, I don't think any of it will have mattered if we don't leave this island."

They reached a door and Mestor tapped out a pattern. "Well, fortunately for you, Professor Gadeiros has a plan."

Pico Airport
Pico Island, Azores
Present Day

Interpol Agent Hugh Reading stepped onto the tarmac, no jetways servicing Pico Airport, and immediately felt the heat. He wasn't a fan of it, though the steady breeze was taking the edge off nicely. His son grinned at him.

"This is perfect. Great idea, Pops."

Reading stared at him for a moment, suppressing a frown.

Pops.

His son had taken to calling him that since he returned from Hendon Police College, where his training to become a police officer was proceeding nicely. He wasn't a fan of the term, though at least it was said in a friendly manner. They had been estranged for years, ever since the divorce, but over the past couple of years, they had both made an effort, and were on the best terms he could remember. Spencer was turning into a fine young man, and Reading couldn't be prouder that he had chosen to follow in his father's footsteps.

And as an added bonus, it upset his ex-wife tremendously.

While it did make a small part of him ecstatic, he no longer held any ill will toward his ex. They had parted on reasonable terms, but his son's refusal to have anything to do with him for years had created a resentment within that he blamed on her. It probably wasn't fair, though it was easier to blame her than himself for not making enough of an effort.

You were the father, he was the child.

He smiled at his son, giving his shoulder a squeeze. "Thank Jim and Laura. This was actually their idea." He scanned the sparse crowd, coming up empty. "Speaking of, where the bloody hell are they?"

"Maybe they're just late."

Reading grunted, heading toward the terminal. "Those two are probably at the bottom of the ocean, exploring their little find, having completely forgotten about the likes of us."

"What *did* they find?"

Reading shrugged. "They wouldn't tell me. Too secret to say over the phone, apparently. The photo they sent looked like some sort of ancient underwater building. Whatever it is, Jim seemed as excited as I've ever heard him, and with the things those two have discovered since I've known them, that's saying something."

Spencer rubbed his hands together. "Nazi gold?"

Reading tossed his head back and groaned. "Oh, don't get me started on that. You know, just a couple of months back, they found a bunch of Nazi gold, but that wasn't even the most valuable thing. They found something called the Amber Room."

Spencer glanced at him. "I've heard of that thing. Why didn't it make the news?"

"Because it was stolen again."

Spencer's eyes shot up. "How?"

"Fancy trucks that can disguise themselves."

"Huh? Like Transformers?"

Reading laughed. "No, I mean curtainsiders with some sort of technology that allowed them to change the advertising."

"Oh, you mean PLED displays?"

Reading's eyes narrowed. "What?"

"Polymer Light Emitting Diodes. Basically, they interweave OLED tech into fabric, and can display a video image on it. Completely flexible and holds up to the usual wear and tear. They're already making clothing from it. Cool stuff."

Reading smiled at his son, impressed. "How do you know about this stuff?"

Spencer shrugged. "When I get my first paycheck, I want to buy the biggest, baddest TV I can afford, so I've been doing some research. Stumbled upon some stories about it. Great if I want my pants to play a movie, but kind of useless for the wall of my flat." He eyed his father. "So, what happened to the gold?"

"I buried as much of it as I could, but I have to wait a while, because I'm probably being watched."

His son's jaw dropped. "Really!"

Reading gave him a gentle slap on the back of his head. "Of course not, you daft bastard. What kind of a man do you think I am?"

"Not a rich one, apparently."

Reading chuckled, continuing to scan those gathered. "Speaking of rich, I still don't see our benefactors."

Spencer nodded. "Neither do I. What should we do?"

"Well, like I said, they're eggheads, so they probably lost track of time." He fished out his phone then dialed Acton's number. It went directly to voicemail. "Hey, it's us, get your arses out of the water and come pick us up!" He hung up and repeated the message on Laura's voicemail, though with a much politer delivery. "Neither are answering, so they're probably a hundred meters under. Let's just get our luggage and head to the hotel. Maybe we'll bump into them there."

He gave one last look about the airport before entering the terminal, wondering why he didn't spot Laura's private jet, nothing parked matching the distinctive paint job sported by her lease-share network.

Could they have left?

Aldeia das Adegas Hotel

Sao Roque, Azores

Hugh Reading handed one of the hotel keycards to his son. "Are our friends here? They were supposed to meet us at the airport, but didn't."

"Names?"

"They would have made the reservations. James Acton and Laura Palmer."

The desk clerk tapped away at her computer then shook her head. "No, I have them out since this morning."

Reading frowned. "Are there any messages for us?"

More tapping. "I'm afraid not."

Reading's frown deepened. "Do you know where we might find them?"

The clerk regarded him for a moment. "Well, normally we're not supposed to say, but since the reservations were all made at once, you're clearly friends. I know we rented a vehicle for them, and I overheard them talking about diving this morning."

"Where might they go for that?"

She shrugged. "I'm afraid you can do that pretty much anywhere. I can get you a list of places that rent equipment."

Reading nodded. "Do that. We'll be up in our room."

"Yes, sir."

Reading and Spencer headed for their room, saying nothing, Reading's cop mind racing with the worst-case scenarios, as his two friends usually warranted it. Spencer unlocked the door and they stepped inside, Reading momentarily forgetting the current situation as he shook his head, the room way out of his budget.

Spencer grinned. "I love that you have rich friends!" He stared at the two beds. "Too bad they didn't get us a suite."

Reading gave him a look. "Don't be greedy. And besides, if they could, I'm sure they would have. My guess is the hotel either doesn't have them, or they were all booked."

Spencer tossed his bag on the bed nearest the window. "Hey, I was thinking. They sent you that photo from one of their cellphones, right?"

Reading nodded. "Jim's."

"Can I see it?"

Reading handed him his phone and his son's thumbs attacked the display. Spencer grinned, handing it back to him, a map displayed with a red dot in the middle.

"That's where it was taken."

Reading's eyes narrowed. "How the hell do you know that?"

"Easy. Most people don't realize it, but when you take a photo, unless you've changed your settings, it geotags it and stores the location in the metadata."

"English, you bastard."

Spencer laughed. "When you take the photo, it stores the GPS coordinates as part of the data." He gestured toward the phone showing the map. "That's where it was taken."

Reading stared at the indicator, surrounded by blue. "According to this, it was taken in the water, which makes sense." He zoomed out slightly and smiled when the coast of the Azores was revealed. "Let's show this to our clerk. She should be able to tell us what dive shops are near there." He put his arm around his son's shoulders and gave him a squeeze. "You're going to make one hell of a copper."

Over the Atlantic

"You're sure your brother won't mind?"

Tark Gerald shrugged at Oswald "Spud" Fletcher. "So what if he does? I'm family, and we need to keep those two out of sight."

Tark buried his head back behind a magazine, leaving Spud to once again look at the posh surroundings they now found themselves in. He had never been on a private jet before, and it was a life he could get used to, though it would be rather hypocritical if he did. He had joined Step Back Now seven years ago, shortly after it had been formed by Gavin Thatcher, and deeply believed in the cause, though for perhaps different reasons than some of the others.

He was chronically unemployed.

And not by choice.

He wanted to work. He struggled to, but as his mother had always said, he didn't "have it all upstairs." He was stupid. He couldn't handle math, he could barely read and write, and he just couldn't concentrate long enough to learn anything useful. He'd had scores of jobs over the years, but few lasted beyond the first week, his employers quickly realizing that eagerness wasn't enough.

When he had bumped into Thatcher on the streets of Liverpool, he had shared his story, and rather than offer advice, Thatcher had given him something better.

A reason.

Computers.

Machines were taking over the world, leaving some people behind, like him. In the days of old, manual labor was in high demand. Shoveling dirt or shit, it didn't matter. A man with a good set of hands and a strong back could always find work.

But not today.

Machines took care of all that. Now all the jobs required the one thing he didn't have—brains. Thatcher had invited him to a speech he was giving, and since he was unemployed, he gave him a listen.

It had changed his life.

Machines were the problem.

Technology was the problem.

Rid the world of these things, and people like him could have a future. He wanted to destroy every single computer that was out there, though that wasn't Step Back Now's goal. Thatcher and most of the others realized that it wasn't the machines that were evil, it was the way they were used. People were forgetting their humanity because of the way they used the technology. Mankind—or peoplekind as he had heard some idiot refer to what most people concerned of such things would have called humankind—would never rid itself of technology, so he'd probably be condemned to the life in which he found himself trapped.

Though it wasn't that bad a life anymore.

When he had finished school, his friends had all moved on, even the lowlifes had jobs. He had been trapped in the same house he had grown up in, constantly berated by his mother, and smacked around by his father every time he came home, fired again.

But now he had friends. Friends who believed in something, and who helped him through not only giving him something to do, even if that was just handing out fliers or holding a gun, but somewhere to live instead of with his parents, and companionship that he hadn't felt in years. Step Back Now was his new family, they were his brothers and sisters, and he would do anything for them.

But kill?

He stared over at their prisoners, as everyone pretended to be business associates so as to not raise the suspicions of the crew of three that manned the plane. Could he kill them if it became necessary? He had never fired a gun in his life. He had thrown plenty of punches, let loose some great kicks, and prided himself on being able to take both— perhaps a few too many to his head when he was younger might explain some things. But kill? No one had ever talked about killing people. That had never been part of the plan.

Never.

They were trying to save mankind. That was why they as a whole had nothing against computers or machines that actually helped people, like medical devices. They didn't want babies dying because incubators were some evil technology. Again, it was how it was used that was their concern. Was it used for good? Or was it used to avoid human interaction? The latter was what they were fighting. Human interaction was what he craved, and it was what everyone should crave.

Human interaction.

He stood.

Tark looked up at him. "Where are you going?"

"Just stretching my legs and taking a leak."

"Well, make it quick. We're landing in Portugal any minute now, and I don't want to waste a second we don't have to."

Spud frowned. "Yeah, yeah." He hated how Tark sometimes treated him like a child. He headed for the rear of the plane then took care of business. He freshened up in the small bathroom, then stepped out, feeling a lot more at ease. As he passed the two prisoners, he couldn't resist the urge, and instead of returning to his seat, he sat across from them.

"Why were you there?"

The man looked at him. "Excuse me?"

"Under the water. Why were you there?"

"None of your business."

Spud tensed, his chest tightening as a rage inside took form. He hated being disrespected. He hated being ignored. He was a person, and deserved better. He tapped his weapon. "You should be more polite, or that woman of yours could get hurt."

The man was about to respond with what Spud was certain would be a threat, when the woman wisely cut him off with a hand and a response. "We're archaeologists. We found something under the water that we were exploring."

All was forgotten, and Spud's eyes widened in excitement as he leaned forward. "Really? You're archaeologists, like Indiana Jones?"

She jerked a thumb at her partner. "He's more Indiana, I'm more Lara Croft."

Spud grinned, his eyes darting to her chest for a moment then back to her face.

Definitely not old Lara. New Lara maybe.

"So what did you find?"

"Just an old city."

"Cool!" His eyes narrowed. "Wait, you weren't far from shore. How come nobody else ever found it?"

The man sighed. "The earthquake shifted the seabed, revealing it."

Spud nodded slowly as he processed this new piece of information. "So another earthquake could bury it again?"

The woman shook her head. "More likely it would slide down deeper."

Spud scratched behind his ear. "I'm not sure what you mean."

The woman put her two index fingers together in the form of the top of a triangle. "The Azores is just a cluster of mountains that happen to be volcanos. Over millions of years they erupted on the ocean floor, and just like volcanos on land, slowly got higher and higher, until eventually they broke the surface of the ocean."

Spud curled his leg up under him. "That's incredible. I had no idea!"

"Most of the islands in the oceans are actually volcanos, like the Hawaiian Islands."

Spud's jaw dropped. "So what you're saying is that if there's another earthquake, the city you found could slide farther down the mountain, toward the ocean floor."

"Exactly."

His eyes widened. "That's why everything was on an angle when we were working! We were on the side of an underwater mountain!"

The man stared at him. "What were you doing?"

Spud froze, realizing he had said too much, but dying to ask one last question, not remembering the last time he had held a real conversation with people, especially people who were clearly this intelligent. "Umm, you said an earthquake could cause the city to slide farther down the mountain. Ahh, what about an explosion?"

Both their eyes widened, and the man leaned in. "Why? What have you done?"

Spud shook his head, panic setting in. "Nothing, nothing, I swear. I'm just curious, umm, there's a military base there, isn't there? You know, explosions from that." He mentally patted himself on the back for the recovery.

The man leaned back, not looking convinced. "If the explosion were big enough, it could trigger another landslide that could send the city sliding to the bottom of the ocean, and beyond our reach."

Spud leaped from his seat. "Yeah, umm, well, thanks for the chat."

The man leaned forward. "If you people are planning on setting off a bomb, then you need to stop what you're doing. You could destroy the most significant archaeological find in the history of mankind."

Spud stared at him for a moment. "Wh-what did you find?"

The two archaeologists exchanged glances, and the woman nodded. The man stared up at him.

"Atlantis."

Professor Ampheres' Residence

Atlantis

Before the fall

Senior Enforcer Kleito motioned for her men to spread out, the pedestrians already blocked, crowds gathering at either end of the street. Nothing annoyed her more than onlookers. Too often, it meant people complaining about excessive use of force, when they had no clue what was actually going on, or shouted questions or protests that tipped off whomever they were after. If it was up to her, she'd arrest anyone who risked her people.

Though the courts wouldn't allow it. Freedom of speech. Too often, it was a notion she disagreed with, but then, how often had she questioned her own political masters in private?

The ground shook again, prompting more questions as she tried to maintain her balance.

If this keeps up, I'm buying a boat.

She loved the sea, a significant portion of her youth spent on friends' boats, sailing around the island nation, or paddling up and down the extensive canals that crisscrossed the city, but she had never been able to afford one of her own. Wood was expensive, a small boat a luxury even for those of means.

And an Enforcer was not someone of means.

She wanted for nothing, her salary decent, even more so since the promotion, but after paying for a roof over her head and food for her belly, there was little left over for luxuries. Yet these earthquakes had her wondering if the conspiracy nuts were right this time.

Shouts from behind the block of homes lining the street in front of her, had her motioning for silence as she cocked an ear.

"They're getting away!"

She cursed at the shouted warning from behind the home, and stormed toward the front door of Professor Ampheres' residence. She kicked it open, the door splintering at the bolt. She rushed into the modest home, her team following her as they pushed through the house, each room checked by the others as she continued through to the back, the door ajar. She looked to the left then the right, and cursed, two of the men she had sent to cover the back, sprinting after someone.

"Let's go!" She took off after them, the pounding feet of her men echoing in the alleyway behind the row of houses. One of her men overtook her then slowed. She glared at him. "Don't you dare slow down for me!"

"Yes, ma'am!"

He took off past her, a couple of the other men doing the same, and it prompted her to redouble her efforts, though her shorter legs were no match for her colleagues. It was an annoyance, but one she could do nothing about, and there was no point complaining about things beyond her control.

She reached the canal to find her team gasping for breath, staring out at the water, two of them sitting on the ground, their faces bloodied.

"What in the name of the gods happened?"

The senior of the two began to struggle to his feet when she waved him off. He smiled gratefully, instead wiping at a seeping wound on his forehead. "When we reached the alley we saw several men running toward the canal with a woman and three children. The suspect's rear door was open, and since the report said he had a wife and three children, we assumed it was his family. We shouted our warning in the hopes you would hear it, and gave chase. As we neared, the men stopped and assaulted us. I'm sorry, ma'am, but we were outnumbered. They bested us, though we got some good blows in, let me tell you, but it was enough to slow us down, and by the time we resumed our pursuit, they had reached the canal and escaped in a waiting boat." His head sagged. "I'm sorry we failed you, ma'am."

She frowned at the two, then stared at the water. "This was well-coordinated, by the look of things. I'm sure you did everything you could." She redirected her attention to their wounds. "Get yourselves tended to, then when the doctors clear you, return to the station. I want descriptions of the men, and the boat."

"Yes, ma'am."

Several of her team helped them to their feet, leading them away as she stepped to the edge of the canal, shaking her head. "Why would they run?"

"Ma'am?"

She glanced at her second-in-command, not having meant to speak aloud. "Just thinking. The family ran, with the help of others. What happened at the Senate wasn't even an hour ago, yet they escaped, with the help of others, who had a boat at their disposal of sufficient size to carry what, ten people?" She shook her head. "That would suggest that Professor Ampheres had planned on stealing Poseidon's Trident all along, but if that were the case, then why not send his family into hiding before he even left?" She growled in frustration. "There's more going on here than we've been made privy to. Somebody else is involved." She spun on her heel, turning to her remaining men. "Send out dispatches. I want the entire city looking for Professor Ampheres and his family. And find me that boat. Somebody must have seen something."

Beja, Portugal

Present Day

One of the advantages, and in rare occasions, disadvantages, of private jets was that they used private terminals. And the security at these was extremely lax compared to the main terminals. It meant that weapons were easily smuggled, especially when personal concierges familiar with the airport staff were whisking their customers through. Searches were rare when the clients were as wealthy as Laura was, which Acton found a convenience, but today, it meant no opportunity to have their captors disarmed by heavily armed security.

In fact, he saw none at the small Portuguese airport they had just landed in. Within minutes, they were in a Jag SUV with a malfunctioning air conditioner and a dash that kept beeping a warning that the owner had bought the wrong car. It was driven by someone he assumed was their lead captor's brother, and the introductions had finally given him names.

Tark and Spud.

Spud seemed almost a simpleton to him, and Tark often showed him little patience. The near childlike wonder displayed during their short conversation on the airplane reminded him of when elementary students would come for a tour of the university. Their questions and jaw-dropping reactions were painfully cute.

In children.

He realized that not everyone was smart. That's why there were measurements like IQ. The median Intelligent Quotient for humans was 100. That meant that half of all humans were above that number, but it also meant that half were below. Spud seemed room temperature. It was sad, really, and probably explained why he had fallen in with criminals, criminals about to explode something near their discovery.

But what? What could they possibly want to destroy under the water off the coast of the Azores? It was literally the middle of nowhere. And if their discovery was indeed Atlantis, which he still had serious doubts about, it might explain exactly why the Atlanteans had chosen to settle there. There would have been no indigenous population, and they could have developed in isolation, without worrying about outside cultures trying to destroy them. They could have focused on peaceful development, rather than constantly preparing for it.

He sometimes wondered what the world would be like if half of it weren't at war, or preparing for war. Every year, the world collectively spent over one trillion dollars on military and intelligence, with the United States accounting for more than half that number. What if just half of that trillion were devoted to science? What diseases could be cured, what problems like poverty or hunger could be solved?

But that was a pipe dream.

With the Chinese and Russians determined to become more dominant than the United States, and with one religion determined to rule them all, he didn't see any future where mankind could live in peace. Hell, even his own country was being torn apart, divided into camps that refused to even listen to the others. Western civilization had devolved into us versus them, right and wrong, with no tolerance for anything in between. Too many people felt that if you didn't agree with their point of view, you weren't just wrong, you were evil.

It was a new development, something he had observed catching on in the past decade, and he blamed social media. When Facebook, Twitter, and other platforms, allowed you to seek out like-minded individuals around the world, instead of in your own community, then become friends with them, you quickly found yourself surrounded by parrots who agreed with everything you said. The platforms then added new "features" that provided you with news stories and posts that they felt would be things you'd be interested in based on your own posts and past "likes."

It was all designed to make you happy, and when you were happy, you stayed on their platform, saw their advertisements, and the companies made money. But the result was that users were caught in bubbles that weren't based upon reality. Many of their friends weren't really friends. They were merely people that agreed with you about the major issues, or even the minor ones. The news stories all supported your beliefs, the shared posts that were actually displayed on your timeline were only those that the algorithms thought would make you happy.

And when that stray person accidentally found themselves in your narrowed field of vision, that stray that didn't agree with you and the hundreds or thousands of like-minded individuals you were "friends" with, you were shocked that there could even exist someone who didn't believe the same as you.

And you attacked.

As a collective.

And you felt good about it, because everyone you knew was jumping on board the same bandwagon, destroying that evil lone individual who dared think something different, because they were obviously wrong. After all, every news story you ever read said you were right. Every friend you had ever made said the same.

It sometimes made him thankful that he and Laura couldn't have children. Who would want to bring someone into this world?

He did hold out some small hope. Some people were beginning to recognize the problem, and some had even approached Apple, demanding they develop a simple phone. If people could just talk, instead of constantly being on social media every waking minute, perhaps then they could realize that there wasn't just right or wrong, but a whole lot of opinions in between, and that those who disagreed with you weren't simply evil or uninformed or misinformed, but entitled to their opinions, and perhaps even correct in them.

He regarded the three men that now held them prisoner, and wondered what had set them off. What bubble had they found themselves in that had created enough rage that they had taken matters into their own hands, no matter the consequences, because those who got in their way, or tried to stop them, were wrong, and perhaps even evil, therefore not worthy of living?

He leaned a little closer to Laura and stared into her eyes, thanking God for every moment they had spent together, and praying that this wouldn't be the end of the purest friendship, and relationship, he had ever had. She smiled at him, and he knew she was completely aware of what he was thinking.

And it made him even more determined to get them out of this situation.

He glanced over at Spud, sitting on the opposite side of Laura, quiet the entire time, and knew he was the key to getting out alive. The man seemed desperate for human interaction, and Acton was determined to give it to him.

And perhaps, with some luck, sway him to their side.

Off the coast of Pico Island, Azores

Hugh Reading had opted for the cheaper dive suits—the ones without the built-in communications gear. They were just too damned expensive, and he wasn't raking in the dough like his friends, though he supposed neither were they. They just had a monster nest egg sitting there thanks to Laura's late brother, and her wise handling of the money after she inherited it. When the dive shop had quoted him the prices, it had made him once again appreciate how much his friends did for him. They had flown him and his son down here, they had put them up in the hotel, and they were paying for all their expenses while here. He was determined to at least work in a dinner on him, just to make himself feel better, but as he had long realized, a vacation to them was a coffee to him, and he wouldn't hesitate to buy them a coffee.

To be rich!

One of the things he liked about his two friends was that they didn't flaunt it. There were no Rolexes or thousand dollar sunglasses. These weren't the Kardashians of the archaeology world, even though they could be. Reading suddenly had a mental image of Acton bent over provocatively with an erupting bottle of champagne, filling a glass perched ever so delicately on his oiled ass. He laughed, nearly spitting out his regulator.

Talk about breaking the Internet.

His son waved at him, about ten feet below, then pointed. He looked and sucked in a quick breath. It was a set of columns, thrusting out of the ocean floor, on an angle that matched the side of the volcanic island that extended out of sight to his right. He kicked hard toward the ruins, thankful for his parents having introduced him to scuba diving during their family trips to Estartit in Spain. He had always been comfortable in the water—after all, he was a Brit—but had also never feared going deep, and a quick glance at his depth gauge told him they were now 180 feet below the surface.

As he entered the ruins, it was clear this was what his friends had been excited about, and he could understand why they might lose track of time. He made as quick a circuit as he could around the periphery, not spotting them, but instead finding several pieces of very modern gear, some of which appeared to be cameras. Someone had been here, and he was confident it was his friends, though where they were now, he had no clue. The fact their equipment seemed intact and functional, suggested this could simply be a matter of bad timing. They might have passed each other on the road here, and could be back at the hotel, waiting for them.

He motioned toward his son then pointed up, beginning the slow ascent. As his mind raced with the possibilities, he inevitably thought of worst-case scenarios, and came to the decision that if he didn't have a message waiting for him on his phone when they reached the surface, he'd ask the dive shops if they had seen them. They would have rented equipment from somewhere, and it was likely from one of the several lining the beach, tourism in the Azores apparently a booming industry.

They surfaced, and Spencer was first in their small boat, hauling Reading in after him. Reading removed his headgear and sucked in several lungsful of fresh sea air.

"That was sooo cool!"

Reading regarded his son. "Now, mum's the word, right? Nobody can know what we saw."

Spencer rolled his eyes. "I'm not an idget."

"You sound like one when you say it like that."

Spencer gave him a look. "Haha." He started up the engine, pointing them toward the shore. "So, do you think that was their equipment?"

Reading nodded. "Probably. I doubt anybody else would have had the time to piggyback on their discovery."

Spencer pointed to a large boat far to their right. "They look well-equipped."

Reading glanced over his shoulder to see a large vessel with a boom lifting a submersible from the water, and suddenly felt inexplicably uneasy. "They're a pretty good distance away from the ruins. I should think that if they had been exploring them, they would have been directly over them like we were."

Spencer shrugged. "We had GPS coordinates to work from, maybe they didn't."

"Well, if they are exploring it, I'm sure Jim and Laura know about it."

Spencer brought them up to the dock and Reading stepped from the boat, tying them off. Spencer handed their gear up to one of the dive shop employees manning the dock, then they both headed for the rental shop.

"Back so soon?" asked the owner, a man they had learned earlier was named Baltasar.

"Not much time, unfortunately. Listen, we had two friends that should have been diving here yesterday and earlier today. Jim Acton and Laura Palmer. He's mid-forties—"

"Yeah, I know them. They rented a bunch of equipment from us yesterday." He wagged a finger at Reading. "I don't like to speak ill of people, but we had to go out and retrieve their boat. They just abandoned it out there when they left."

Reading tensed as his eyebrows rose. "Wait, you saw them leave?"

"Yeah, they came back on another boat with two others, then left."

"When was this?"

Baltasar shrugged. "A few hours ago, I guess."

"Any idea where they went?"

"No idea, just that they went that way." Baltasar pointed down the road, leading toward Sao Roque and the hotel.

"Did you find anything in their boat?"

Baltasar shook his head. "No. I hope they left their valuables in the car, because the boat looked like it was picked clean when we found it."

Reading frowned. "Picked clean?"

"Well, there was nothing on board except some of our tanks. None of their personal stuff."

"And they took their car?"

"Yes."

Reading frowned, then handed him a card. "If you think of anything else, call me. My cell number is on the back."

The man took the card, his eyebrows shooting up his forehead. "Interpol! Are they in some kind of trouble?"

Reading frowned. "I hope not."

Professor Gadeiros' Residence

Atlantis

Before the fall

Ampheres stepped through the door, Mestor's hand pressed firmly on his back, urging the reluctant professor forward. The interior of the home was dark, all the windows covered, any lighting extinguished. The door closed behind him, completing the effect. He heard the distinct strike of a fire starter and a spark lit the room with a brief flash before a lamp emitted a dull glow.

"Okay, quickly people, let's not keep our guest in the dark too long."

Ampheres heard feet shuffling before he made out the silhouettes of those acting upon the orders of a voice he could never forget, but hadn't heard in years. He was grateful for the few moments of privacy, steeling for the encounter about to come. Curtains were moved aside behind him, allowing the light to flood in from the overhead windows, the lower windows still covered for privacy's sake. He blinked several times, then stared at his former mentor, Professor Gadeiros, unsure of what to do.

Gadeiros had no such indecision.

He stepped toward him, his arms extended, a broad smile on his face. "My, how you've matured!" He embraced Ampheres, giving him a thumping hug, as if the rift between them had never existed, and Ampheres had merely been off on some journey for the past ten years.

"I, umm, it's, umm, good to see you, Professor."

Gadeiros eyed him. "Are you sure?"

Ampheres' eyes shot wide, his jaw dropping before snapping shut. Gadeiros tossed his head back, roaring with laughter.

"You should see your face, my old friend." He motioned toward a chair, Ampheres finally noticing the other half-dozen in the room, all young, possibly students of the esteemed professor. He sat, his old mentor sitting across from him. "Your presentation didn't go well."

Ampheres grunted, folding his arms. "No, I should say not."

"I thought you presented your findings quite well, and your insults were well-timed. Stealing Poseidon's Trident was a foolish ending, however."

Ampheres' eyes narrowed. "Were you there?"

Gadeiros nodded. "In the gallery. I had heard you were presenting, and wanted to hear what you had said."

Ampheres glanced at Mestor. "I understand you presented your own findings recently?"

"Yes, and they too fell on deaf ears, I'm afraid. I had hoped when one of the most respected academics of the city backed up my findings, perhaps those fools would listen, but your actions, I'm afraid, have negated anything you said."

Ampheres stared at his former mentor, dumbfounded at the words. "Most respected academics? Was someone else presenting today?"

Gadeiros laughed, the others in the room joining in. "My young friend, do you still think so little of yourself after all these years? Your accomplishments are well-known throughout the city by those who should know of these things, and I have followed your career with pride, if not some shame."

Ampheres' eyes narrowed. "Shame? What could you possibly be ashamed about?"

"How I treated you. I let your relationship with my daughter, and its unfortunate demise, destroy *our* relationship. I should have been able to separate the two, but unfortunately, I couldn't. My daughter was hurting, and you were already dating someone else. I protected my daughter, rather than my daughter and my apprentice." He sighed. "The heart is a foolish organ, is it not?"

Ampheres grunted. "You won't get any argument from me." He lowered his eyes. "How is, umm, your daughter?"

"She is well. She married, as I'm sure you know, and has two children of her own. It is a good match, a better match than I fear you two would have made, as are you and your wife."

Ampheres' eyes widened and he leaped to his feet. "My wife and children! I have to go get them!"

Gadeiros raised a hand, urging him back into his seat. "Why?"

"They're in danger! If the Enforcers are after me—"

"They are after you, not your family. We are a civilized society. The worst that may happen is that they are taken in for questioning, then released this evening. They've done nothing wrong, and the law knows that."

Ampheres dropped into his seat. "But they'll be worried." He shook his head. "I have to make sure they're okay."

Gadeiros leaned forward and patted Ampheres' knee. "Not to worry, my friend. My people have already moved to secure them. You shall be with them shortly."

Ampheres' hammering heart continued to pound, not calmed by Gadeiros' assurances. "I don't understand. What is going on here?"

Gadeiros sighed. "The end of the world, if your findings, and mine, are to be trusted."

Ampheres took several deep breaths, trying to calm his heart. "I still don't understand. What is going on? Why have you brought me here? Why have you taken my family?"

Gadeiros smiled gently at someone behind Ampheres.

"He's trying to save your life, silly."

Ampheres leaped to his feet, his eyes wide as he turned to stare at the first woman he had ever loved. "Leukippe! I, umm, I—" He sighed, his shoulders slumping, his chin dropping to his chest. "I have no idea what to say."

Leukippe, as beautiful as ever, stepped closer, placing a hand on his chest, patting him gently. "'Hello' might be a good start."

He lifted his chin slightly, staring into her eyes, his heart slamming once again, this time with a shame he hadn't felt in years. "I think 'sorry' might be better."

She smiled then suddenly thrust into his arms. He returned the hug, then felt her push away slightly, and he let go. "It's so good to see you." She gently smacked him on the cheek. "That's for being a foolish boy."

He smiled, his cheeks flushing. "I deserved much worse."

She tapped his chest. "And believe me, ten years ago you would have gotten a good thrashing, I assure you. But you were right, we weren't right for each other. We were both in the relationship for the wrong reasons. Though it was painful, we both ended up where we should have."

He smiled, relieved. "I'm happy to hear you say that. I've felt horrible all these years for what I had done. I'm pleased to hear you have made a wonderful life for yourself. Children, I hear?"

"Yes. They're already on the boat, with my husband, but I wanted to be here to see you when you arrived, just in case you tried anything foolish like refusing to come with us."

Ampheres' eyes narrowed. "I don't understand." He turned toward Gadeiros. "You still haven't told me why I'm here."

"I brought you here to save your life, and to save Atlantis."

Aldeia das Adegas Hotel

Sao Roque, Azores

Present Day

Reading sat on the edge of his bed, waiting for his son to finish a ridiculously long shower, taking the time to make some calls. He was on hold, listening to some Muzak, when Laura's travel agent Mary, came back on the line.

"Sorry for the wait, Mr. Reading, but I've just confirmed that their charter departed over two hours ago."

Reading suppressed a curse. "Are you sure? They were supposed to meet us here earlier today."

"I know, that's what's odd. I made your flight arrangements as well, and Mrs. Palmer was quite clear that you and your son were joining them. That's why I had you on hold for so long. I've reconfirmed with the pilot himself that the Actons, along with two guests, were on board, with a last-minute flight to Portugal. Beja Airport, to be specific."

Reading frowned. "Portugal? Why the bloody hell would they go there?"

"I'm sure I don't know. Should we, umm, be concerned?"

"Where is their plane now?"

"Still there."

"I'll need the pilot's number."

"I don't think I can give you that."

"Don't think of me as a customer asking, think of me as Interpol Agent Hugh Reading asking."

"Oh, umm, I forgot what you did, sorry. Okay, I'll get that number and call you back right away."

"Thank you." Reading ended the call just as the shower turned off. He stared at himself in the reflection of the television for a few moments, unhappy with what he saw.

You're getting too damned old for this.

He sighed, his entire body feeling the years it continued to pile on, and his shoulders sagged as a wave of self-pity swept over him.

Keep it together, you old bastard. Your friends are depending on you.

And he had no doubt they were. There was absolutely no way they would leave the country without at least sending a message, and he had reconfirmed that not only were there none left at the front desk, but there were no emails, voicemails, or text messages anywhere. They had left with no notice whatsoever.

He tweaked upon a thought that caused his jaw to drop slightly. They *hadn't* left the country. The Azores were an autonomous region of Portugal, so any flight would be treated as domestic if it landed in Portugal. That meant less security at the airport, which if they were being held captive, would mean less chance of his friends seeking help.

He needed to track them, and he needed to track them fast, before they were moved. He could use his Interpol resources, but they might take too long. There was only one person he knew who wouldn't be affected by red tape, because red tape simply didn't apply to him. He pulled out his phone and sent the message.

Now he had to hope it was received in time.

EQ Hotel & Casino

Shanghai, China

CIA Special Agent Dylan Kane gazed with appreciation, and a bit of guilt, at the bevy of beauties parading past him, his host, Zhang Qi, a Chinese arms dealer, commenting on each one's sexual proclivities and unique talents, all, Kane was sure, in the lead up to having him pick which one—or ones—he wanted to spend the night with.

It wasn't so long ago that this wouldn't have bothered him in the slightest. In fact, it might have excited him, but now that he was in a serious relationship, he found it difficult.

Which is why serious relationships are discouraged.

He had never been in love before, except perhaps for some teenage hormonal infatuations that were mistaken for love, but now that he was, he kept picturing his girlfriend, Lee Fang, hugging her pillow and sobbing at finding out that he had been unfaithful.

Yet that wasn't the reality.

He had already been forced to be unfaithful as part of the job, and it had eaten him up inside until she had finally confronted him, demanding to know what was wrong. He had told her, and she had been fine with it. Perhaps no other woman would have, but with her having been Chinese Special Forces, she understood the business, and didn't fault him for it.

He wasn't sure he'd be so forgiving.

He loved Fang with all his heart, so much so it was painful to be away from her, yet most days that was the case. As a covert operative, assigned to mostly work in Asia, he was rarely home—there was almost always a mission.

Like tonight.

Zhang was a known arms dealer, selling advanced Chinese weaponry on the black market to people who shouldn't possess such things. Kane, using his cover as an insurance investigator for Shaw's of London, was here to investigate an insurance claim placed by the notorious criminal for the theft of his $50 million yacht.

A yacht Kane had a team steal a week ago.

In reality, he was here to steal the proof of what Zhang had been up to, so it could be passed on to the Chinese, who would shut down his network selling pilfered military assets.

Zhang had insisted on pleasure before business, Kane was sure in an attempt to make him more willing to rule in his host's favor, after doubts were raised with respect to the insurance claim. The night of booze, drugs, and hookers was drawing to an end, with Zhang shitfaced, and Kane pretending to be. He *was* drunk—you could only spill so many drinks without it becoming suspicious—but he had avoided the drugs, except for a few joints that had made the rounds.

A finger was raised, and the women that had been parading in a circle for the past half hour, stopped. Zhang leaned toward Kane. "Choose."

Kane feigned ignorance. "Excuse me?"

"Choose. Which one do you want to take back to your room?"

Kane's eyes widened slightly, then a smile spread across his face. "Only one?"

Zhang roared with laughter, tossing his head back and slapping Kane on the back, his entourage of heavily armed guards joining in. "I like you, my friend!" Zhang waved at the women, all of whom had smiles plastered on their faces, some seemingly genuine, some forced. "Pick as many as you want."

Kane chuckled, shaking his head. "I'm afraid I'm not as much of a man as you are. I'll limit myself to one, thanks." Kane had already chosen which one he wanted, but for a very different reason than Zhang was expecting. He searched the group for the one whose eyes had betrayed her, the one who seemed the saddest of the bunch, who clearly didn't want to be here.

He found her, her artificial smile heartbreaking. He pointed. "Her."

The woman trembled, the smile breaking for a moment.

"She's yours!" Zhang shoved him forward. "Now go! Have some fun, and we'll talk business in the morning!"

Kane stood, pretending to wobble slightly, eliciting more laughter from his host, then approached the poor girl, taking her arm and leading her to the elevator, hoots and hollers following them. They boarded the elevator and he hit the button for the penthouse level, no expense spared by his host. "What's your name?"

"Tien."

"A pleasure to meet you. I'm Dylan."

"I-I know."

He smiled at her, but made no attempt to even touch her with a comforting pat on the shoulder. The doors opened and he led her to his suite, holding the door open for her. She stepped inside and headed for the bedroom without hesitation, apparently having been here before.

"Wait."

She turned, her eyes wide with the fear of having upset him, something he was sure would result in some sort of punishment for her should Zhang find out. "Did I, umm, do something wrong?"

He smiled gently, shaking his head. "Not at all." He sat on the back of a couch facing the floor to ceiling windows providing an impressive view of the city below. "Can I confess something to you, Tien?"

Her shoulders rolled inward. "Umm, yes?"

"I have a girlfriend."

Her eyes widened, but she said nothing.

"So, if you don't mind, how about we just order some food, watch some television, then go to sleep?"

Her jaw dropped. "You mean no jiggy-jiggy?"

His smiled broadened. "No jiggy-jiggy. Just two friends watching a movie and enjoying a meal."

Her shoulders slumped and an audible sigh escaped. "I-I think I'd like that."

Kane stood. "Great! Let me get changed into something more comfortable, and why don't you, as well?" He motioned toward her revealing outfit that looked a little too tight in several key areas. "There are robes in the bathroom if you want."

She nodded. "Okay."

Kane headed for his bedroom as Tien went to the second bathroom. He stripped out of his suit, moaning with relief as he removed his shoes then tie. As much as he liked dressing up in the monkey suit, he preferred sandals, shorts, and a loose shirt whenever possible. He changed, and as he was about to rejoin Tien, a mild electric shock pulsed from his watch and into his wrist.

He cursed.

He stepped onto the balcony, leaning against the far left edge where there was a blind spot in the camera coverage identified earlier by part of his support team posing as a cleaning crew. He pressed a coded sequence into the buttons on the side of his CIA-issue watch, then read the message that scrolled across.

Not again!

It was from Interpol Agent Hugh Reading, which could mean only one thing. The professors were in trouble yet again. He chuckled, shaking his head.

It's a wonder those two are still alive.

He fished out his phone and made an encrypted call to his former Archaeology Professor's friend.

"Hello?"

"Hey, Agent Reading, this is Dylan. How are you?"

"How do you bloody well think I am?" Kane smiled. "Those two have gone and done it again. It looks like they've been kidnapped and taken to Portugal."

Kane's eyes narrowed. "Kidnapped? How so?"

"They were supposed to meet us at the airport, but they never showed. I questioned their dive equipment supplier, and he said he saw them leaving with two men. I confirmed with Laura's travel agent that the plane, with them and the two men, left unexpectedly, and landed at some small airport in Portugal."

Kane pursed his lips. "Portugal? Why there I wonder?"

"They were in the Azores, so I'm guessing because it would be a domestic flight, so fewer questions."

Kane's head bobbed with this little tidbit of essential information. "Okay, that makes perfect sense. What do you want from me?"

"I'm heading to Portugal now with my son. I'll contact my office, but I need to know where they went, and fast. No red tape and intergovernmental liaising crap delaying things."

Kane grinned. "Then I think I've got your man. Expect a call shortly."

Leroux/White Residence, Fairfax Towers

Falls Church, Virginia

CIA Analyst Supervisor Chris Leroux leaned back on the couch, enjoying the show. His girlfriend and first real love, CIA Agent Sherrie White, was parading to and from the bedroom as she tried on different outfits, trying to find something that his mother would be pleased with.

"How about this one?"

Leroux took the time to let his eyes roam her body from toes to nose, then nodded. "Perfect."

She frowned. "You said that about the last one."

He shook his head. "No, I said that about the last *six*. Stop worrying. Now that they know what you and Dylan do, you're gold. You saved their lives."

She beamed. "I guess I did do that, didn't I?" She disappeared again, then strode out naked save a hat perched atop her head rather than covering any naughty bits. "Ya think I could get away with a birthday suit?"

Leroux felt a soldier rising to attention. "I think my father would probably like it."

Her eyes widened. "Eww!" She eyed his shorts. "Well, I know *someone* who likes it."

He adjusted himself. "I have no idea what you're talking about."

"No?" She sashayed forward, licking her lips. "Are you sure you don't know anyone who likes what they see?"

Leroux groaned as she leaned forward, the girls on full display. "I think I might have an idea or two."

"Two? Kinky!"

Leroux's phone demanded his attention on the couch beside him, but Sherrie paid it no mind, continuing her show, full mast achieved. He glanced at the call display and groaned again. "It's Dylan."

Sherrie stopped, hands suddenly on her hips as she looked around. "His timing is way too suspicious."

Leroux rolled his eyes. "Tell me about it." He grabbed the phone and swiped his thumb. "Hey, Dylan."

"Hey, buddy, am I interrupting anything good?"

Sherrie bent over and kissed her fingers then smacked her ass. "Did you see that, Dylan?"

"Huh?"

"Sherrie's convinced you've got cameras here."

"Of course I do, but don't tell her."

Leroux tensed. "Umm…"

Kane laughed. "Oh God, I wish I could see your face. Wait, I can!" More laughter. "Just kidding, buddy. No cameras, but if Sherrie wants me to see something, just take some pictures."

"Yeah, that's not gonna happen."

"Ooh, must be good ones then."

Sherrie dropped to her knees in front of him, giving him a sly look. *She's so awesomely bad!*

"I'm kind of in the middle of something. What do you need?"

"Can't a friend just call his buddy?"

"A buddy would realize when to call back later."

"*Definitely* something good. Fine, the professors are in trouble again. Agent Reading just called me. It looks like they've been kidnapped by two men and taken to Portugal from the Azores. I've sent all the details to your encrypted email. Can you give them a hand?"

His fly was unzipped. "Sure, I'll get the team on it." Something was gripped. "Gotta go!"

"You dog, you!"

Professor Gadeiros' Residence

Atlantis

Before the fall

"Please tell me you've figured out a way to stop it!"

Professor Gadeiros stared at him, his expression reminding him of years ago, when Ampheres asked naïve questions of his teacher. He finally spoke. "I fear Poseidon himself couldn't save us, even if he were willing."

Ampheres frowned, leaning back in his chair. "I never thought I'd see the day when you of all people would look to false gods for help."

Gadeiros grunted, waving at the cracked walls surrounding them. "Desperate times, my friend. No, I don't believe in the gods, but part of me does pray for something or someone greater than us to save our people, for I know no mere mortal can."

Ampheres sighed. "Then what is your plan to save Atlantis?"

"You're conflating two different concepts. Don't you remember your own speech?"

Ampheres' eyes narrowed as he stared at his mentor, drawing a blank. "I'm afraid my impassioned plea fell on the deaf ears of an ignorant Senate, but of my own as well." He gestured toward the trident sitting on the table. "Remember, I *was* acting quite irrationally."

Gadeiros laughed. "You said 'Atlantis is its people,' and you were right. It isn't this city. Cities can be rebuilt. I intend to save Atlantis by saving enough of its people and its knowledge so that we can rebuild after the coming calamity passes."

Ampheres' heart raced, his eyes widening. Had his mentor accomplished what he hadn't? Had he somehow convinced their leaders to prepare for evacuation of as many as possible? His eyes narrowed. That would be impossible. If Gadeiros had succeeded, then why the resistance shown today by the Senate. He glanced at his old love, then at her father. "How many?"

"Fifty."

Ampheres' shoulders slumped at the pitiably low number, his heart aching as his stomach flipped. "Fifty." His voice was barely a whisper. "Surely we have to do better." His eyes filled with tears as his head sank between his knees. "We *must* do better."

"I'm afraid all we can hope is that our demonstration tonight will convince some to follow us, but we're lucky to have what we do. I had to lie to the university to get the research vessel we now have. I've had copies of as many of our historical and scientific texts moved on board, along with enough supplies to get us back to the mainland. I have chosen the students very carefully, a mix of young men and women, who will help rebuild our society when we find a new home, if they are unable to return here."

Ampheres lifted his head, wiping the tears away with his fingers. He felt Leukippe's hand on his shoulder and he looked up at her, giving her a weak smile. Her touch brought back a flood of wonderful memories, and for a moment, he almost forgot he was a husband and father. It felt so familiar being with them, so comfortable, Leukippe, her father, and a younger version of himself having spent so much time together, it was easy to forget the days of pain that ended the years of joy.

His heart skipped a beat as he picked up on something his old mentor had said. "They?"

Gadeiros' eyebrows rose slightly. "Excuse me?"

"You said 'if *they* are unable to return here.' Don't you mean, we?"

Gadeiros shook his head. "This is a young man's expedition, not an old man's. I will remain here, and try to get as many on the boats as I can when the time comes, but I will not be going with you."

Ampheres leaped to his feet, his hands clasped behind his head. "Out of the question! You must go! It's your plan!" He began to pace, then spun with a thought. "You *have* to go! You yourself said they were all students. Who's going to lead them? Surely you don't expect mere students to rebuild our society!"

Gadeiros smiled at him again, again with that look that had always made him cringe when he was younger. "I have no intention of leaving them leaderless."

Ampheres opened his mouth to respond then stopped when he realized what his former professor meant. His jaw snapped shut and he began to shake his head, his hands joining in. "No, surely you don't mean…" He dropped into his vacated chair.

"I can think of no better choice." Gadeiros leaned forward. "You are young enough to lead them for decades, until they too are old enough to have learned the lessons of a life lived. You are well respected, and the most gifted student I ever had the privilege to teach. Those I've handpicked know of you, know my opinion of you, and have all sworn to me that they will obey your commands." Gadeiros rose, and Ampheres stared up at him, his mind a jumble of thoughts as he tried to process everything that had just been said. "My pupil, my friend." Gadeiros held out both hands and Ampheres took them, rising to his feet. "My equal."

Ampheres stared at him, then grunted. "I'd hardly say that."

Gadeiros squeezed his hands. "I see you still underestimate yourself." He let go of Ampheres' hands then wagged a finger at him. "If you are to be the founding father of the second incarnation of our great civilization, then you'll have to show more confidence in yourself."

Ampheres shook his head. "I can't do it."

Gadeiros' expression hardened. "You *must*. There is no time to choose another that I trust. *You* are the one."

There was a coded knock at the front door and Leukippe opened it. Ampheres breathed a sigh of relief as his wife and children were ushered inside. He turned to greet them when Gadeiros grabbed him by the shoulder, swinging him back around. "Remember what you have to lose." Gadeiros leaned closer, lowering his voice. "If you don't do this, there's no room for you on the boat. Or them."

Ampheres' chest tightened as a rage built within. He wrested his shoulder from Gadeiros' grip. "You would play god with the lives of my family?"

Gadeiros shook his head. "If those students don't have you to lead them, then they are as good as dead. I'm sparing your family that tragedy, and granting them the quick death of those who will be left behind." Gadeiros' expression softened and he placed his hands on Ampheres' shoulders once again, gently, staring up into the taller man's eyes. "Be the man I need in this hour. Be the man our people need. Save yourself, save your family, save my daughter and her family, but most importantly, save Atlantis from itself."

Somewhere over the Atlantic

Present Day

Konstantin Kozhin leaned back in his chair and put his $10,000 Louis Vuitton clad feet up on the state of the art console, at least from a Russian perspective, and closed his eyes. They burned from the dry air and the constant vigil of the past twelve hours, but it would soon be over. All the charges were in place save one, and with the push of a button, he could detonate any or all of the transatlantic data cables that stretched across the ocean floor between Europe and North America.

Every day, 99% of international data passed back and forth on these cables, carrying everything from phone calls to emails between individuals, corporations, and governments, most sent by people painfully unaware that the cables even existed—most thought everything was transmitted via satellite once it left their continent, but that simply wasn't true. Less than half of one percent of data went through satellites, the bandwidth necessary to transmit everything, simply far too expensive to do non-terrestrially.

And what he had planned would disrupt communications between the two continents significantly, possibly for months. Yes, the cables would be repaired, new ones perhaps laid for additional redundancy, but not only would it take time and money to fix the problem, it would cost the economies potentially billions due to the disruptions, and perhaps cause people to question their dependency upon the bandwidth they took for granted.

Yet all of that only mattered to those to whom he was *not* the benefactor.

The Luddites he was associated with were trying to change the world, and he was merely trying to change *his* world. They were useful idiots, like many activists, who had grand dreams but no money to fulfill them. It wasn't until the Soros of the world began funding activists, that they gained any press or traction. They were pawns on a chessboard they couldn't possibly understand, manipulated by the very wealthy elite they disdained, all pushing agendas that would make their minions' skin crawl.

Though to compare himself to the master, would give himself too much credit. Even he could admit that. He had money, left to him by his father, and it was dwindling rapidly. But when he had overheard a conversation in a bar in Manchester after a football game, it had piqued his interest, and he had asked to join the table.

That was when he met Gavin Thatcher. Thatcher was smart. Brilliant even. And passionate in his beliefs. If he had gone into politics, he might have even been successful at it if he could have toned down the rhetoric, though that wasn't to be his destiny. Thatcher was determined to change the world, had grand plans to do it, but no money. Kozhin had the money, but no interest in saving the world—it wouldn't die off before he did, leaving him determined to enjoy life to its fullest in the here and now. It would be the next generation that had to deal with the mess, and the rich could live without the petty problems brought on by society's crises.

Though it was something Thatcher had said that had him truly intrigued. When he had spoken about the problems with social media, he found himself agreeing in general with what he was saying, thinking of his own friends list on Facebook, and how he barely knew any of them. Thatcher's idea to try and disrupt the Internet, if only temporarily, was intriguing, yet impossible, as far as Kozhin was concerned.

But it turned out that wasn't completely true.

While within nations the redundancy of the design was robust, it was between continents that it wasn't. The underwater cables. They sat, unguarded, on the ocean floor. Most who even knew about them dismissed tampering because of the depth, but those few were ignoring the fact that the seabed at either end was merely a shoreline.

A beach.

The depths were zero feet at the ends.

Thatcher's fantasy was cutting these cables to disrupt the flow of data, and perhaps getting people to lift their heads for even a few days, just so they could see the world around them. It was a noble fantasy, but with Kozhin's connections, not a fantasy at all. His father was not a good man, or rather, hadn't been a good man. He was dead. Dead in a single vehicle crash on the roads outside of Moscow. It was blamed on alcohol, though what the authorities hadn't known, was that his father had recently been diagnosed with liver failure, so hadn't touched a drop in months.

No, his father was murdered by the Russian president-for-life, because he had dared to challenge him in a newspaper interview. He was dead within days, and most of his assets frozen, only to be seized over the coming months. Leaving Kozhin only what he had managed to hide before the hammer dropped, his father always warning him to keep a rainy day fund.

With what he had left, and with his connections in the desperately corrupt Russian elite, he could bring Thatcher's plans to fruition, but for entirely his own reasons. Destroying data cables could send a temporary message. *Threatening* to destroy data cables could send a lot of money into his offshore accounts.

A *lot* of money.

There was a knock on the door and he sighed, sitting up. "Come!" The door opened and one of the contractors he had hired stepped inside, snapping to attention as he had been trained to before going private.

"Sorry for the interruption, sir, but we have a radar contact approaching."

Kozhin frowned. "Who?"

"A flight of American F-15s, we believe."

Kozhin rose and peered out one of the small windows at the crisp blue sky of 36,000 feet. "Have they challenged?"

The man shook his head. "No, sir. We don't expect them to. We are in a Russian Air Force plane, over international waters. As far as they're concerned, we're merely a curiosity."

A smile crept up one side of Kozhin's face. "Tell your commander, his idea of running this operation from the air was brilliant."

A smart salute was snapped. "Yes, sir!"

Kozhin dismissed him with a wave of his hand. "Keep me informed if they do anything out of the ordinary."

"Yes, sir!"

"And send the communique."

The man smiled. "Yes, sir!"

He left, closing the door behind him, and Kozhin returned to his chair, leaning back once again and closing his eyes as the hum of the Ilyushin Il-80 airborne command and control aircraft he had blackmailed a very corrupt Russian general for, lulled him into a light snooze, visions of the billions he would have before the day was out, raining before his eyelids.

Operations Center 3, CIA Headquarters

Langley, Virginia

Chris Leroux stood in the middle of the state of the art operations center, his team of nearly a dozen hard at work on their latest tasking. Data was already pouring in which seemed to confirm the two archaeology professors were indeed missing. It had already been confirmed that they had left their hotel that morning as expected, but never returned. Satellite imagery showed their rental off the coast of Pico Island, then docked hours later, corroborating somewhat the story provided to the Interpol agent by the dive shop. Most importantly, their private jet, part of a lease-share network, had filed a last-minute flight plan, leaving the islands ahead of schedule, and landing in Portugal less than two hours ago. Their phones were off, and had been for most of the day, and beyond a text message from Palmer's phone to her travel agent requesting the flight to Portugal, there had been absolutely no communications with them.

"What do you make of that?"

Leroux glanced at Randy Child, a genius level hacker with no brain-mouth filter. "What?"

Child pointed at the displays wrapping around the front of the op center then tapped his keyboard. A satellite image of the Azores zoomed in on a rather large vessel compared to the pleasure crafts in the area. "Looks like they've got some pretty serious equipment there."

Leroux stepped closer, his head slowly bobbing as Child focused in on an expensive looking submersible on the rear deck. "Could be anything."

Child nodded. "True, but didn't Agent Reading say they were diving in the same area?" He tapped his keyboard again, bringing up photos from the past twenty-four hours, showing the ship anchored in the same position, the submersible not on board in the earlier photos. "They've been there quite a while, obviously doing something underwater. Maybe they saw something."

Leroux smiled. "Good thinking. Get the registry, let's see if we can make contact."

"Sir?"

Leroux turned toward another of his analysts, Sonya Tong. "What have you got?"

"Footage of them arriving in Portugal." She gestured toward the displays, bringing up security camera footage of the professors and two men leaving the airport.

"Good work. Let's run their faces, see if we can identify who their friends are. And tap every camera in the database. I want to know where they went."

"Yes, sir."

Outside the Senate Chambers

Atlantis

Before the fall

Senior Enforcer Kleito stood along the sidelines of the protesters, dozens of students chanting at the steps of the Senate, demanding to be heard. Their message was clear. They agreed with the nutbar Professor Ampheres, who had escaped her clutches earlier in the day.

But that wasn't who they were chanting about. It was another man she had never heard of, academia not an interest of hers. She had gone straight to the Academy, and never looked back, always knowing what she wanted to do with her life for as long as she could remember. She wore plain clothes now, and she stared longingly at the crisp uniforms worn by those lining the steps, creating a human wall, protecting their government from any who might threaten it.

The protest was peaceful so far, but as it continued, and more joined them, she feared it might not remain so. People were scared. The earth was shaking at least once an hour now, the steam from the mountain was constant, yet the criers in the squares, delivering the latest messages from the various government departments, continued to proclaim there was nothing to fear.

She didn't believe them anymore.

But she had her orders, and she had to follow them. If the government did have a plan, it could only be executed if law and order prevailed, and if it didn't, as these protesters insisted, then all would be lost, and it would be up to her and her fellow Enforcers to maintain order, rather than let Atlantis descend into chaos in its final days.

The students were rallying around a man named Gadeiros, an elderly professor who had given a rousing, well-spoken speech, that had many of her fellow Enforcers exchanging nervous glances.

And it had tipped her opinion on the debate.

Yet it made no difference. There were tens of thousands of Atlanteans. There were boats enough for maybe a couple of thousand, and most of those could never survive the trip to the mainland. If these people were right, they had to act now and save as many as possible, and if they were lucky, and time was on their side, perhaps those boats that made it to the mainland could return and save more.

The ground trembled again, as if to tell her it was impossible.

She searched the crowd for Professor Ampheres, a copy of his official portrait having been sent over earlier from his university. She was quite certain he wouldn't be here, but with the message delivered matching his, she had to wonder if he had planned to be here, those plans scuttled by his idiotic theft of Poseidon's Trident.

This was not a bad man, just someone who had let his frustrations get the better of him, and normally she would have expected him to turn himself in, with the trident and an apology. But instead, his family had been retrieved, her men had been assaulted, and what had seemed relatively innocuous once she had the facts, now seemed much more sordid.

She spotted a man speaking to the elderly Professor Gadeiros, a man with a bandaged nose and two black eyes, who also met the general description of one of those who had assaulted her men earlier.

We got some good blows in, let me tell you.

Could this be one of them? A man belted in the nose recently, matching the description given by her men, talking to a professor who held the same beliefs as her suspect?

She didn't believe in coincidences.

She stepped into the crowd, her plain clothes allowing her to blend, and her relatively young age not making her stand out too much among what was still mostly students, though there was a significant contingent from the general public now on the periphery, listening earnestly to what those working the crowds had to say.

Their message was getting out.

She glanced at the Senate.

But I doubt it's getting in there.

She made her way closer to Gadeiros and his wounded companion, when the professor raised his hands, silencing the crowd. "It is time." And with those few words, the crowd broke, and he and the bandaged man headed for the canal, apparently to catch a transport. The crowd parted, letting their distinguished leader on the platform first, and there would be no way to join him without using her identification and thus defeating the purpose.

She eyed the canal and spotted a small government transport bobbing gently against the stone edge. She rushed toward it and flashed her ID at the pilot. "I need your boat."

He shrugged. "That's what I'm here for."

She pointed at the transport ahead of them as it pulled away. "Follow that."

"Yes, ma'am." He attached to the powered line and the small craft lurched ahead, sending her tumbling into her seat. She didn't bother chastising the man, the urgency in her own voice to blame, and instead sat back and enjoyed the ride.

She loved riding the canals, and often wondered what it must have been like before the transportation system had been created. The canals were ancient, but the concept of rapid transit using waterpower instead of manpower, was only about a century old. Massive waterwheels at the end of each line constantly spun, keeping the lines moving at a near steady speed. Leads from the boats were simply clamped on and off, and the boats moved at a reasonable speed that allowed anyone to get pretty much anywhere in the city within half an hour. The worst that ever happened was a line breaking, and there were crews stationed throughout the city to respond immediately. It was an ingenious system that had allowed the city to spread even farther from its core, and had nearly eliminated horses from the streets. She had never ridden one, their numbers now greatly reduced, most relegated to the fields and forests, used for labor rather than transporting people.

The transport slowed ahead, and her pilot disengaged from the powered line, bringing them to a halt along with other boats in the queue. Normally, a boat like this would simply disconnect and glide by, the pilot on the tiller expertly guiding them past, but not today, which made them somewhat conspicuous.

She leaped to her feet, spotting the professor and his companion disembarking. "That's them." She stepped onto the platform then rushed up the steps to the main street, searching the crowd in the fading light, soon spotting her subjects. She tailed them through the thinning crowds, the slower pace of the elderly man making her all the more conspicuous, especially after a couple of streets were passed and they were in a residential section. Fortunately, she was trained, and trained well.

She managed to avoid being made, and was soon smiling as the two men entered a rather nice residence, large enough to suggest means, though plain enough to leave little doubt substantial wealth did not live behind the walls. She saw a curtain move, as if someone were checking the street for pursuers, then nothing.

She strode toward the home, casually, its façade directly on the sidewalk, as were all the homes along this street, any courtyard to be found in the back. She slowed to as relaxed a pace as she could without being obvious, and strained to hear any voices from inside.

And had to suppress a smile at the first words she heard.

"I was beginning to worry!"

"Ampheres, my old friend, you have bigger things to worry about than my wellbeing."

Kleito didn't bother listening to any more. She had them. But she was only one, and she had no idea how many lay beyond that door. She noted the address, then headed for the canal and its MessageStream. A few minutes later, she removed her Enforcer key from around her neck and unlocked the emergency access point. She quickly scrawled a note, then rolled it up, placing it into the brightly colored emergency tube, then dropped it into the fast flowing water. She closed the access hatch then locked up the station, rushing back toward her target's hideout.

Backup will be here soon!

East of the Azores, Atlantic Ocean

Present Day

Gavin Thatcher smiled at the others as they gathered for lunch. "We did good today, my friends. Very soon, when people bury themselves behind their phones, they're going to discover that they can't contact a lot of their friends, that things just might get so slow it won't be worth trying, and when our bots finish their job, our message to the world will be the number one most trending video on every single social media network."

"From your lips to God's ears!" Giselle raised her glass and grinned. "And hopefully She's listening!"

Thatcher laughed then raised his glass. "Hopefully!" He took a drink then sighed. "I never thought we'd see the day." He raised his glass again. "To Mr. Kozhin, the reason we've been able to do so much!" The glasses were raised again, though not as enthusiastically.

His eyes narrowed as he looked about the table at the people he considered his closest friends in the world. "What's wrong?"

Giselle lowered her chin, her eyes darting about the room. "Well, umm, I don't want to speak for anyone else, but can we trust this guy?"

Thatcher's eyebrows rose, and he motioned at their surroundings. "Without him, we'd have none of this. We'd still be sitting in your flat, wondering what we could do with no resources to change the world."

She nodded. "Yes, well, while I don't deny that, just think about it. We're talking about a man who obviously has a lot of money, and clearly questionable friends."

Thatcher's eyes narrowed. "What do you mean?"

Giselle leaned forward, staring at him. "Ahh, hello? Explosives? Detonators? How the hell did he get those things? We were so eager to accomplish our goals, we never sat back and asked whether the price was worth it. We know almost nothing about this guy, and beyond that first meeting in Manchester, none of us has even talked to him in months."

Thatcher raised a finger. "I've talked to him almost every day."

"Yes, and that's all well and good, but you've been so blinded by this opportunity, have *you* even stopped to think about it for a moment?" She pointed out a porthole. "Hell, we've taken prisoners today! And to top it off, you left them with two morons!"

Tarrell Fleming grunted. "Better than having those idiots handling the explosives."

Chuckles reluctantly emerged around the table at the muttered comment, and Thatcher smiled. "They'll be safe, don't worry. As soon

134

as our message is delivered and the explosives are detonated, they'll be set free, since it will be too late."

"But they can identify us!"

Thatcher shrugged. "So? We all approved the message I recorded, and it names our organization. We haven't exactly kept a low profile on the Internet. The authorities are going to identify us regardless, and probably within minutes. They'll eventually capture us, and when they do, it will give us another platform in which to spread our message. If we pull this off, and detonate all these transatlantic cables, our arrests will be front-page news for weeks, and our trials will be for months. People will be forced to listen to our message, and the governments won't be able to stop us."

Giselle frowned, her shoulders slumping as she leaned back in her chair. "Yeah, I suppose you're right. I guess part of me just hoped we'd get away with it."

Thatcher shrugged. "Who knows, maybe we will. We're not exactly going to hand ourselves over, are we?"

The comm panel on the wall squelched. "Thatch, I've got a strange call for you."

Thatcher's eyebrows shot up as he rose and pressed the *talk* button. "Who is it?"

"They're claiming to be from some university, looking for two missing professors."

Thatcher tensed as faces around the room paled. "Wh-what have you told them?"

"Nothing, I said I'd see if you were available."

His heart hammered hard. "Did you give them my name?"

There was a pause. "I-I might have said 'Captain Thatcher.'"

He closed his eyes as his pulse pounded in his ears. "Put them through."

"Yes, sir."

There was another squelch.

"This is the Captain."

"Hi, Captain Thatcher"—his head slumped—"my name is Chris Leroux. I'm calling from St. Paul's University in Maryland. We had two of our colleagues diving in your area this morning, and they're now missing. We were wondering if you might have seen anything."

Thatcher forced several deep, slow breaths. "I'm, uhh, not sure why you think we would have."

"Well, they were in the same area you were this morning."

Thatcher's eyes narrowed. "How do you know where we were?"

"Oh, nothing clandestine, I assure you. The dive shop noticed your boat in the same area, and provided the name of the vessel. Then it's just a few quick calls to actually reach you. So, did you see anything that might help us?"

Thatcher leaned his head against the cold metal wall, his eyes closed. "No, I'm afraid we didn't."

"Okay, thanks for your help. Leroux, out."

A final squelch signaled the end of the call, and Thatcher slowly returned to his seat.

"What the hell just happened?" asked Giselle.

Thatcher shook his head. "I'm not sure, but there's no way that was a university looking for their people."

Giselle stared at him. "What makes you say that?"

"Because it's only been a few hours. There's no way they should even know they're missing yet."

Operations Center 3, CIA Headquarters

Langley, Virginia

Leroux turned toward Randy Child. "So?"

Child spun in his chair, a hand raised in the air, a finger pointing at the ceiling. "He's lying!" He dropped a foot, bringing his spin to a halt, then pointed at the display showing the stress indicators in "Captain Thatcher's" voice. "He was definitely lying about something, and since you pretty much asked him only one thing, I think it's safe to say he knows what happened to the professors."

Leroux agreed. "That's my read too." He pointed at the boat. "Okay, run down everything you can on that boat, and see what we can find about this Captain Thatcher." He turned to Sonya Tong. "Any luck in Portugal?"

She nodded. "I've got them getting into a vehicle. I ran the plates and it belongs to an ex-pat named Zek Gerald, currently residing in Portugal. I'm running him down now."

"Excellent work as usual."

Tong blushed, her crush on her boss apparently still in full bloom.

"As soon as Agent Reading lands, get that intel to him."

"Yes, sir."

The door to the ops center hissed open and National Clandestine Service Chief Leif Morrison rushed in, staring at the displays then turning to Leroux. "Are you still working on the missing professors?"

"Yes, sir. Making some progress, too."

Morrison waved a hand. "Leave it with your team, I need you."

Leroux's eyes narrowed. "What's going on?"

"Something big. Priority briefing with the White House, right now. I want you there."

Leroux gulped. "Umm, okay." He followed Morrison toward the door. "What's it about?"

"We just received a ransom demand, and I need to know if it's complete bullshit, or if what they're threatening is actually possible."

East of the Azores, Atlantic Ocean

Thatcher and the others sat around the table, an array of laptops opened and connected via satellite to the main news sites around the world, along with constantly refreshed Facebook and Twitter trending lists.

And nothing was happening.

"Shouldn't we have heard something by now?"

Thatcher nodded at Giselle. "I would have thought so. When I spoke to Kozhin and told him we had finished, he said he'd be sending our message shortly, then detonating all the charges."

"Maybe we should go back, see if it detonated."

Thatcher shook his head vigorously at Giselle's suggestion. "Absolutely not! If it did go off, then us sailing back into the area will just deliver us into the hands of the authorities, and if it didn't, then something has gone wrong, and perhaps the authorities are already there."

Tarrell Fleming jabbed a finger at the comm panel. "I think that guy who called you is behind this. I bet he was CIA or something."

Thatcher gave him a look. "Riiight. The CIA is looking for two missing professors. That makes absolutely no sense."

Fleming shrugged. "Well, whoever he was, knows your name, so you better hope he doesn't pass it on to the authorities."

Thatcher tensed and everyone at the table tore their eyes away from their screens, staring at him.

Giselle cleared her throat. "Maybe we should let them go? That way whoever it was will have no reason to keep asking questions?"

Fleming dismissed her suggestion with a derisive grunt. "They were still kidnapped! There's going to be questions, no matter what. We can't let them loose until we know the charges have detonated, and the message has been delivered, so that way they can't stop us."

Thatcher closed his eyes, his optimism rapidly draining. Something was definitely wrong. If the cables had been detonated, and the message delivered as Kozhin had promised, then they should have heard something by now. He stood.

"I'm calling Kozhin."

Conference Room 212, CIA Headquarters

Langley, Virginia

Leroux sat against the wall, only the senior staff sitting at the table, a grid of monitors showing dozens of other faces jacked into the meeting with the senior administration officials, the big man himself absent.

White House Chief of Staff Nelson kicked things off. "For those of you who are unaware, we received this message only minutes ago."

The displays switched to show the silhouette of a man's face, superimposed on an image of an underwater scene showing several people doing something to what appeared to be a cable of some sort. A computerized voice spoke.

"This message is for the American President. Over the past week, teams under our employ, have placed explosive charges on over a dozen transatlantic data cables. These charges are large enough to completely sever the connections, and severely inhibit the ability of

142

North America and Europe to communicate electronically. Should you doubt our sincerity, please check the status of the TAT-14 cable. You will find it was destroyed at the same time this message was sent."

The image paused, and Nelson appeared for a moment on the screen. "We have confirmed that this connection has been severed, though we don't have confirmation yet that it was physically severed or if this is some sort of digital block."

The silhouette reappeared, the recording resuming. "I won't bother explaining all the ramifications, as I'm sure you have experts who can explain them to you. The repair of these cables will take time, and will be quite expensive, however the damage to your economies will be in the billions. Again, you have experts who can explain this to you." The silhouette moved closer, revealing no additional identifying details. "Our demands are simple, and a mere token compared to the true cost to your economies. You have two hours from the time this message was sent, to transfer one billion American dollars into the account number we have attached to this message. If we do not have the full amount in our account within two hours, we will detonate another cable, and the price will double. Another two hours, and the process repeats, and the price again doubles. We highly suggest you don't delay, as quite quickly the price will rise to an amount even *you* can't hide from the public. Oh, and Mr. President, if you try to disarm any of the bombs, I will know, and the price will again double."

The message ended, and the display returned to the grid of attendees. Leroux was already firing a message to Randy Child when

Morrison leaned back in his chair and turned toward him. "What do you think?"

Leroux's phone vibrated.

Confirmed.

"I've just confirmed the cable is down. I think we have to take him seriously."

Somebody overheard him. "What if it's only one cable? And what if it's just a hack?"

Morrison leaned forward, addressing the room. "How long will it take to determine how the cable was severed?"

"It depends on where the break happened," replied somebody from the monitors.

Leroux cleared his throat. "We should be able to quickly determine where the break is—that capability is built into the system. Then a visual inspection should confirm the method."

Somebody guffawed. "You do realize how long that cable is? How deep it is? Who is this idiot?"

Leroux's cheeks and ears burned. Morrison glared at the monitors. "That idiot is a hell of a lot smarter than you could ever dream of being, Director. I suggest you listen to him, because one day he's probably going to be sitting in this seat." Leroux flushed even more. Morrison turned to him. "You were saying?"

Leroux's mouth was suddenly dry, but he pushed through. "Unless we're dealing with someone who has access to a military grade submarine, then I doubt we're talking significant depths here. And if we aren't, then the device shouldn't have been placed too far from shore.

Once we determine where the break occurred, I'm guessing local authorities could be on site before the deadline."

Morrison smiled slightly at him then turned back to the display. "Do you want to get real answers, or continue the name-calling?"

There was silence for a moment before Nelson took back the meeting. "We'll move forward with your suggestion, Leif. In the meantime, we have to assume that this individual is serious, and decide what to do about it."

The Chairman of the Joint Chiefs shook his head. "We can't pay the money. We don't negotiate with terrorists."

Morrison grunted. "We all know that's bullshit. We're always negotiating with terrorists, we just do it through third parties."

The head of Homeland responded. "Yes, but who do we use this time? We've got two hours before he detonates again."

The CJCS waved a hand, as if dismissing everything said. "Assuming this wasn't a one-off. Perhaps we should wait and see if he's bluffing."

Morrison frowned. "An expensive bluff. I suggest the money be pulled together so that it can be transferred if that decision is made, pull up our scenarios for this type of situation, as I'm sure someone has thought of this before, and then the President and his team can decide whether or not the economic fallout is worth paying the man. In the meantime, we'll try to figure out who he is, and stop him before he gets a chance to detonate more of these cables."

Nelson agreed. "Sounds good. We'll reconvene in one hour."

The meeting broke and Leroux followed Morrison out of the room.

"I want your entire team on this."

Leroux nodded. "Understood."

Morrison paused, raising a finger. "I'm not sure you do. Your *entire* team. That means the professors' problems aren't even on the back burner."

Leroux suppressed a frown. "Yes, sir."

Professor Gadeiros' Residence

Atlantis

Before the fall

"Everybody is talking now. They can't hide it anymore."

Ampheres stared at the man, Mestor, who had saved him earlier. "That may be, but we know it's already too late." As if to emphasize his point, the ground shook once again, the tremors coming more frequently, as if the earth were about to give birth to something horrible. "If we don't evacuate now, there may be nothing left." He stared at his mentor, Gadeiros. "I wish you would reconsider."

The old man shook his head emphatically. "I still have my reputation, and that may count for something in the coming days. I will continue to voice my warnings, and hopefully, some will heed them and save themselves. But you must leave now and join your family and mine on the boat. There is no more time to waste. You must set sail the moment you arrive."

Ampheres' shoulders slumped, his heart still hammering with the pressure of what was being asked of him. A few months ago, the tremors and steam were a curiosity, something to be investigated, not feared. He was a professor, a husband, a father. Not the savior of Atlantis. If he were, shouldn't *he* have been the one to put together an expedition to save his people? No, Gadeiros should be the one to lead them, but the old man was determined to be a stubborn fool.

Old man.

Ampheres regarded his mentor for a moment, noticing for perhaps the first time just how gray the man's hair was, how wrinkled the skin, how hunched the shoulders. He hadn't seen him in so long, he had been seeing the man of a decade ago instead of the feeble figure he had become. His mind was definitely there, but the spring in his step was long gone, and he likely wasn't long for this earth, certainly not if forced to live those last days on a perilous journey to save civilization. He frowned, and his mentor smiled.

"You realize I'm right, don't you?"

Ampheres' eyebrows rose, his eyes widening slightly. "You appear to still know me better than I know myself."

Gadeiros chuckled. "I have a few decades more experience in reading people than you have, my friend." He leaned forward, patting Ampheres on the knee. "Don't worry about me, my friend. I will continue to spread the message, and when the time comes, I will sit in my courtyard, a glass of wine in my hand, and toast the apocalypse, beside the grave of my wife, content in the knowledge that you and the others will rebuild after we are gone. And with a clean slate, who knows, perhaps what you create will be even greater than what our ancestors accomplished."

Ampheres drew in a deep breath then exhaled loudly. "You do realize that this amount of pressure does no one any good. I fear you will still be grading me from the afterlife."

Gadeiros laughed, tossing his head back. "I just might!"

Mestor held up a finger, silencing the two men as he made for the window. He pushed the curtain aside slightly, then cursed. "The Enforcers are here!"

Ampheres leaped to his feet, holding out a hand for Gadeiros, who waved it off, turning to Mestor.

"You know what to do."

"Yes, Professor." He bowed. "It has been an honor."

Gadeiros smiled. "The honor has been mine. Now, I ask you to place your faith in my apprentice, and protect him as you have me."

"You have my word."

Gadeiros turned to his former student. "Tell my daughter and grandchildren that I love them."

Ampheres' eyes burned and his chest ached as he struggled to control his emotions. "I shall." He didn't bother to ask this man who had once been like a father to him, to change his mind. There was no point. And no time. He bowed, closing his eyes, then felt Mestor's hand on his arm.

"We must go, now."

Ampheres nodded and followed Mestor to the rear of the house, glancing over his shoulder to see Gadeiros lean over and pour another glass of wine.

I'm sorry it won't be in your courtyard, my friend.

Mestor shoved aside a cabinet, a passageway revealed behind it, as someone hammered at the front door. "Hurry!"

Ampheres stepped into the passageway, Mestor following before pulling the cabinet closed behind them. A torch was lit a moment later, and Mestor led the way, the shouts of the arriving Enforcers fading behind them.

Goodbye, my friend.

Zek Gerald Residence

Outside Beja, Portugal

Present Day

Acton tested the zip ties binding his hands, and kept his disappointment hidden. They were tight. Too tight. That not only meant they were cutting into his skin, but that they'd be extremely difficult to break. He rocked slightly in the kitchen chair he was strapped to. It creaked.

Good. Break the chair, and your hands and legs are free.

It told him these men weren't professionals. Real pros would have bound their hands and ankles together, and left them on the floor with a guard. These men had strapped their hands and feet *individually* to rickety chairs. Unfortunately, there was a great equalizer in the entire situation.

Two of them, in fact.

Two handguns, tucked into the belts of their original two captors. The third, who had met them at the airport, was conversing with them in hushed, angry tones in the next room. Apparently, the third man, named Zek, wasn't too pleased with the unexpected houseguests.

"What were you thinking involving me in this?"

"I'm sorry, Zek, but I had no choice."

"Yes, you did. You could have gone anywhere in the world but here. And you should have warned me! Now I'm on camera having picked you and them up. The authorities are going to come looking for me!"

Spud spoke up meekly. "Umm, maybe we should leave. You can say that you didn't know, and immediately kicked us out."

Tark growled. "Shut up!"

"No, don't shut up. That's the first intelligent thing I've heard said here today. You should leave. Now!"

"But where are we going to go? It's just for a few more minutes, I promise. Once we see the first news reports that it's happened, then they'll be set free."

"And I'll still be blamed."

Tark appeared in the doorway. "You two getting all this?"

Acton shrugged.

"Would you tell the authorities the truth about my brother?"

Acton nodded. "Absolutely."

Tark disappeared. "There, see? You've got nothing to worry about."

Acton winked slightly at Laura. Zek was now no longer a threat, and Spud was still malleable, in his opinion.

"Fine. But if I don't hear this announcement within one hour, you're all out of here regardless."

Tark walked past the doorway. "I don't understand why we haven't heard anything. They were supposed to detonate the cables over an hour ago. Something must have gone wrong."

Acton's eyes widened, as did Laura's. "Hey, what are you guys detonating?"

Tark reappeared. "Shut up!"

"Listen, like I told your friend, we were surveying a new archaeological site that was just discovered underwater, off the coast of the Azores. Not far from where you captured us. If you're planning on detonating a bomb or something, then you need to stop. The entire site could sink even farther."

Tark's eyes narrowed. "What kind of site?"

"An ancient city."

His eyes widened. "In the Azores? Bullshit."

Acton forced a chuckle, hoping to keep the conversation going. "That's what I thought, but it's there. And there's significant evidence to suggest it might be the lost city of Atlantis."

Tark's eyebrows shot up, and Zek appeared at his brother's side. "Are you serious?"

"He never kids about archaeology," replied Laura.

Zek stepped into the kitchen. "I thought Atlantis was just a myth."

"So do most people. So did we. This could be the first physical evidence that it actually was real."

Zek sat across from them. "And if my brother's bomb goes off?"

"It's not *my* bomb, it's the group's."

Zek dismissed his brother's protests with an annoyed flick of the wrist.

"The city is on the side of the volcano that makes up Pico Island. Yesterday's earthquake caused a landslide that revealed part of the city. An explosion could cause the entire city to slide farther into the ocean. Far enough, and we may never be able to properly explore it, or perhaps even find it."

Zek stared up at his brother. "If this is true, then you have to stop what you're doing."

Tark's eyes bulged. "Are you kidding me? We're trying to save the future! Who cares about the past?"

"Bah! I've listened to your nonsense for years, and you've accomplished nothing beyond posting some YouTube videos."

"That was before we had money. Now look at us!"

Zek gestured toward the next room where CNN International was playing. "Look at what? You claim you've placed explosives on the transatlantic data cables, and that they should have already been detonated. Would you even recognize a bomb?"

Tark's mouth opened for a rebuttal, yet nothing came out as he apparently began to have doubts. "Umm, well, no. But I'm sure somebody would."

Zek shook his head. "Who in your merry band would? How do you even know that any other charges were placed?"

Tark jabbed at the air between them. "*That* I do know. We personally placed four charges, and three other teams placed the rest. I know everyone on those teams, and we've been in constant communication. I know the charges have been set."

Zek shook his head. "Yet here we sit, with CNN talking about nothing, like they usually do." He rose, stabbing Tark's chest with his forefinger. "One hour, then you're all out of here."

Operations Center 3, CIA Headquarters

Langley, Virginia

Leroux entered the op center, tense, hating what he was about to do—order a halt to their efforts to locate the two missing professors.

"Hey, boss, found them."

Leroux suppressed a grin, but a smile still escaped as he walked toward Randy Child's workstation. "Good work."

Child spun, his arm in the air, then stopped, the arm coming down dramatically, a finger extended toward Sonya Tong. "Not me. The credit goes to the lovely lady in green and black."

Tong gave him a look. "It's teal." She gestured toward the screen. "I was able to trace the ownership, and we've got an unsecured camera on a neighbor's house. The car is in the driveway."

Leroux suddenly didn't feel as guilty. "Okay, excellent work people." He bowed slightly to Tong. "Sonya." She smiled, looking away. "But we've got new orders. Package up everything you found and send it to Special Agent Kane, along with the non-classified stuff to Agent Reading. They'll have to run with it from here. We've got bigger fish to fry."

Tong attacked her keyboard as the rest of the room turned their attention to their boss.

"I just got out of a briefing. An unknown individual or group has just delivered a video message to the White House. They're claiming they have just blown up one of the transatlantic data cables, and are threatening to detonate one every two hours, unless we pay them one billion dollars in less than"—he checked his watch—"ninety minutes. Then the price doubles each time."

Child swung in his chair. "I've reconfirmed that the TAT-14 cable is down."

"Any idea where?"

"Yeah, less than a mile off the coast of France."

"Good, that matches my suspicions, so hopefully the assho—sorry, gentleman—who thought I was an idiot, is answering his door tonight, because I'm having UberEats deliver him some crow."

Child raised a hand and Leroux high-fived him without missing a beat.

"All the intel we have has been sent to your terminals. Start going through it. I want to know if there's anything in the video that might identify who actually sent it, where it was recorded, where it was sent from. Check satellite imagery to see if we can spot anything suspicious around the data cables, specifically around the one we know has been severed. Let's do our thing, people, and solve this before anyone else does. Just imagine the Christmas bonus this year for saving the world once again."

Laughter spread through the room as everyone knew there were no bonuses, and they were underpaid compared to the private sector. But that didn't matter here. Everyone loved their job, and most would do it no matter what the pay was. Those who cared about such things either never took a government position, or left within a few years once they realized the opportunities here weren't money, but power. His boss had said something in today's briefing that had stunned him, and terrified him.

One day he's probably going to be sitting in this seat.

Did Morrison actually think that one day he'd be the Chief? He still hated being an Analyst Supervisor.

But did he?

He looked around the room, everyone's head down, doing their jobs, executing the orders he had just given. Nobody questioned him now. He had proven himself despite being younger than many of them. He no longer dreaded entering an operations center or a team meeting.

Holy shit! You're actually enjoying this!

He sat at his terminal at the center of the room, a slight smile on his face. It was the first time he had realized the fear was not only gone, but that he was comfortable in this position he had been thrust into, kicking and screaming, by Morrison.

But Chief?

Never. But then again, in another twenty years, who knew?

Ugh! Twenty years! I'll be an old man.

He'd be approaching fifty. It was something he couldn't even imagine.

"Looks like the message was received through a Russian civilian communications satellite before it hit our terrestrial network."

Leroux looked at Child. "Can you trace it past that?"

"I'm trying, but it gets trickier with each jump."

Leroux rose. "Show me where the satellite was positioned when the call went through it."

A map appeared on the display, the satellite shown with a cone of coverage projected on the surface of the globe. "It's geostationary. This one covers the northern hemisphere, mostly the North Atlantic, Arctic, Siberia. Top of the globe stuff."

Leroux grunted. "Civilian my ass. Anything unusual from the Russians within the coverage area?"

Tong turned toward him. "Do you really think the Russians could be behind this? This could be considered an act of war."

Leroux shook his head. "I doubt the Kremlin is involved, but that country is so corrupt, nothing would surprise me."

Child grunted.

"What?"

"Well, the Russians are up to all kinds of things, but they're all pretty normal, except for one thing."

"What's that?"

"We've got a Russian Ilyushin Il-80 over the North Atlantic that's been flagged."

Leroux's eyes narrowed. "What's so unusual about that?"

"It's apparently just flying in a big circle, and has already been refueled at least once. A P-3 Orion noticed it, so they've been monitoring from a distance. Some F-15s were sent in to provide support just in case the Russians decide to play any games."

Leroux's gut told him this was important. He had no proof, but he never ignored his gut, and neither did his bosses. It was what had him in the big seat now. "Can we get eyes on it?"

Child nodded, shots from the F-15s and the Orion appearing.

Leroux watched for a moment. "Have they been challenged?"

"They were asked if they needed assistance, and were told no, and to back off. That's it. Wait."

Leroux tore his eyes away from the footage. "What?"

Child was listening to something, a finger poised in the air. "Okay, another aircraft is entering the area. It's a Russian Ilyushin Il-78."

Leroux's eyes narrowed. "Refueling aircraft? Again?"

"That's what's being reported."

Leroux shook his head. "Why the hell would they have a plane circling over the Atlantic, long enough that they'd need to refuel it multiple times?"

Child shrugged. "Got me, boss. Could this have something to do with it?"

Leroux shook his head. "I still can't believe the Russians would do this, but those are definitely Russian military"—he gestured toward the screen—"or at least that one is. We'll soon see if the other is."

"Just a sec." Another feed appeared, one of the aircraft having broken off to cover the new arrival. "Looks Rooskie to me."

"Okay, pull the tail numbers, find out what we know about these aircraft. Are they legit? Where are they based? Everything."

EQ Hotel & Casino

Shanghai, China

Dylan Kane hated to admit that he was having a good time. As soon as he had eliminated the expectation of sex, the young Tien had calmed, and after a couple of hours, became comfortable. Room service had been ordered and eaten, desserts now enjoyed, as they sat in separate chairs, laughing at 22 Jump Street on Pay Per View with Chinese subtitles. Their conversation had been minimal, since he didn't want to get her in any trouble. He was sure the room was bugged, and he stuck to character for the same reasons. What little conversations they did have, surrounded favorite foods, movies, and music—the safe things. No discussions of where she was from, or her family.

She seemed like a wonderful, nice girl, who would probably make a great wife if she hadn't been forced into working for Zhang Qi. It broke his heart, because in so many ways she reminded him of his girlfriend when he had first met her. Desperate, with no options but to accept help from a stranger. Part of him wanted to save this poor woman, but he couldn't. Too many lives were at stake.

Tonight, the cameras would be overridden, allowing him to go out on the balcony, and up the side of the building to the roof of the luxury hotel owned by Zhang, where he'd tap their data lines. Langley would pull the information they needed off his server, he'd remove the tap, and return.

Hopefully undiscovered.

Then tomorrow morning, he'd continue with his cover, the boat would turn up in Macao, and it would be over. Dylan Kane, insurance investigator for Shaw's of London, would depart that afternoon.

I wonder if I should ask for a parting gift.

He glanced at Tien. He could perhaps arrange for her to return to her family, at least.

But what if it was the family that sold her into slavery?

His watch pulsed again, demanding his attention. He entered the code and read the message. Leroux. Which meant it was urgent. He rose, and Tien began to follow. He smiled, waving her down. "I just have to use the bathroom. You keep watching."

She nodded, her eyes glued back to the screen, her four scoops of ice cream gripped in her hands forgotten. He headed for the bedroom and closed the door. He used the bathroom then grabbed a cigarette, something he only ever did out of necessity, and used it as an excuse to go on the balcony once again. He pulled up the encrypted message and frowned.

Let's hope Agent Reading can handle things.

There was nothing more he could do from this end, and the message indicated the location of Acton and his wife had been forwarded to the Interpol agent. All that was left was to pray that they weren't moved before Reading's flight landed, and that he could get local help in a timely manner.

He fired the agent a message, indicating to contact him if he couldn't get assistance. If needed, Kane would send some of his contacts to help. It wasn't his preferred method of resolving this, as it would probably mean bodies and cover-ups, but he wasn't about to let the professors be harmed because of red tape.

I wonder what could have had them pulled off the assignment.

He checked his phone's newsfeed and saw nothing of significance. Whatever it was, it wasn't public. He flicked his cigarette over the side, then cursed at himself for using the world as his ashtray.

East of the Azores, Atlantic Ocean

"There's been a technical problem. The satellite we're using to communicate with the detonators went into a maintenance cycle. We can't risk sending it from another satellite, because we could be traced."

Thatcher pulled at his hair, his eyes closed. "How much longer?"

"We're not sure, but it should be any minute. We're being refueled shortly, so don't worry about it."

"Refueled?"

"Never mind, nothing you need to concern yourself with. Besides, the later in the day on the east coast of the United States, the better. We'll make the supper hour news."

"Okay, just keep us posted. People are getting jittery here."

"Tell them not to worry. As soon as the satellite is back online, we'll be sending our message and the detonation codes. I have to go, but I don't want to be contacted again. It's too risky."

Thatcher tensed. "Umm, okay. How will we know?"

"Just watch the news."

The signal went dead, and Thatcher tossed his headset onto the console. Something was wrong. He didn't know where Kozhin was located, but if it needed refueling, it sounded like an airplane.

We're being refueled shortly.

It had to be a plane. If it were a boat, there's no way they'd need refueling already, and if it were a truck or some other sort of vehicle, you just pulled up to the pump and refilled the tank. He had assumed Kozhin would be in a building somewhere, not mobile, but perhaps being mobile was safer. In the air might, in fact, be brilliant.

He shook his head. He didn't understand the ins and outs of satellite communications, so he had to take the man's word for it. It made sense that there were maintenance modes that could interrupt communications.

He rose, a pit forming in his stomach, as he tried to figure out what he should tell the others.

Beja Airport

Beja, Portugal

Reading stepped off the airplane with Spencer, his phone rapidly vibrating with multiple messages. He checked to see there were several from his partner, Michelle Humphrey, back in London, plus two that he recognized as encrypted. He logged into the secure messaging service Kane had given him access to, and found a message from the Special Agent, and one from Langley's Leroux. He read Kane's first, and cursed.

"What?"

He glanced at his son. "They've been taken off the case. We're on our own."

"Who?"

He gave him a look. "Don't be daft."

Spencer suddenly caught on. "Oh, right."

Reading quickly read the attached file, and grunted with satisfaction at the address and GPS coordinates provided. He brought up the CIA message which was mostly a repeat, without the offer of less than legal help at the end.

His phone rang and he smiled at his partner's caller ID. He swiped his thumb. "Reading."

"Oh, good. I just saw you landed, so I took a chance. Have you heard anything new?"

"Yes, I've got an address."

"How'd you manage that?"

"You don't want to know."

"You and your mysterious sources. Anyway, I've got good news. Lisbon is cooperating. Local police should be meeting you at the airport."

"Umm, Pops?"

Reading looked at where his son was pointing, several uniformed officers rushing toward them. "Yeah, I think I see them now. You're sure they're not about to arrest us?"

Michelle laughed. "If they do, call your friends to post bail."

"Haha. If you don't hear from me in the next ten minutes, send out a search party." He ended the call and put on his most pleasant of faces. The man in charge, short with an impressive beer belly and a sweat covered brow, snapped out a quick salute.

"Are you Agent Reading of Interpol?"

Reading nodded. "I am."

The man gestured at Spencer. "And this is?"

"My assistant."

"Very good. I am Chief Ventura of the Polícia de Segurança Pública."

"Pleased to meet you. I have a location on our kidnap victims."

The man's eyes widened, an excited smile shared with his compatriots. "Excellent news! We will leave at once."

They followed the small entourage through the airport, their escort making a show of shouting for the thin crowds to get out of the way, Ventura clearly one who reveled upon the small amount of power he possessed.

It made him nervous.

Three squad cars were waiting outside, filled with men, none of whom appeared properly equipped for an assault.

"Are your men trained for this?"

Ventura laughed. "Absolutely. Just tell your friends to keep their heads down when we get there." Laughter erupted from the cars, a little too much eagerness visible in the eyes. Reading sighed as he climbed into the back seat of Ventura's car.

It might have been better to get Kane's people.

Professor Gadeiros' Residence

Atlantis

Before the fall

Senior Enforcer Kleito stepped inside the residence she had tracked her suspects to after the all-clear had been announced by her men.

And found herself disappointed.

"Is this it?"

The head of the assault team nodded. "Yes, ma'am. He's the only one we found."

She shook her head, her eyes wandering the room as the old man continued to nurse a glass of wine. "I saw another man arrive here with you, and I heard Professor Ampheres speak."

The old man stared up at her. "My companion left, and I'm afraid I haven't seen Professor Ampheres in over a decade." He shrugged. "We had a bit of a falling out, you see."

She stopped her examination of the room for a moment, eyeing the liar with disdain. "See, that is the problem with people who aren't accustomed to lying, Professor. They take it too far. I could have believed that your companion left, because I too had to leave to call for backup. But by denying that Professor Ampheres was here, when I know he was, it makes everything you tell me suspect." She twirled her hand over her shoulder, keeping her eyes on Gadeiros. "Tear the place apart if you have to. They're here, or they had some way out of here that let them get past our men out back."

The old man's eyes darted toward the rear of the house and she smiled. She leaned closer, turning her head toward where he had looked. She spotted a large cabinet against the wall in the next room. "I wonder what's behind that."

The old man paled slightly, then recovered, taking another sip of his wine. "Nothing but dust, I'm sure."

"And why don't I believe you?" She strode into the next room and grabbed the cabinet by the corner, pulling on it. It didn't budge.

The old man laughed. "I had it bolted to the wall when the tremors started. You won't be moving that any time soon."

She frowned, one of the younger Enforcers snickering. She ignored him, instead turning her attention to the floor. And the wide arc cut into the dust that covered the tile, left behind by the numerous earthquakes and the damage inflicted to the ceiling. She pointed at the floor. "Now doesn't that look odd?" She stepped back. "Rip it off the wall if you have to."

Two of her men stepped forward, apparently eager to break something, tearing at the wood of what must be a very expensive piece of furniture. It didn't take long before it suddenly broke free from the wall, revealing a hidden doorway drenched in darkness. She flicked her wrist, the men stepping out of her way as their chests still heaved from the destructive effort.

"Light."

A torch was lit and handed to her, the shaped polished stone surrounding the tip causing the reflected flame to form a beam of light that stretched into the darkness, revealing a set of stairs. The ground suddenly shook, fiercely, and she struggled to maintain her balance as the walls around her cracked, the floor at her feet splitting several inches before things settled.

"There isn't much time."

She spun toward the old man. "Then why resist?"

"Who's resisting?"

"Why are you protecting him?"

"Because he was the closest thing to a son I ever had."

"But he's a thief!"

Gadeiros shook his head. "No, he's desperate. Everything we know is about to be destroyed, and our government does nothing about it."

"Obviously they don't agree with you."

The old man rose, striding toward the window at the rear of the home, an immaculate courtyard visible through the opening. He pointed to the mountain in the distance that dominated the skyline.

And she gasped.

Harsh reds and oranges now streaked its sides, and a dark plume of smoke regurgitated into the sky. It was unlike anything she had ever seen. "What is it? What's happening?"

"We're not sure, but our scouts have told stories of mountains that erupt with fire and ash, and that consume the lands around them, absolutely nothing but the sea able to stop the onslaught."

She couldn't tear her eyes away from the sight, her team gathering beside her, the fear in the room palpable. "What are you saying?"

"I'm saying, as Professor Ampheres has been saying, that Atlantis is already lost, and that everything that we were, or will be, will soon be obliterated."

"Surely we can escape? We have boats!"

"Yes, some will, hopefully, but too few, and completely unorganized. That is what we have been doing here. Planning for our future. Ampheres will lead a group to sea, and they will return when this calamity is over to rebuild, or find a new home if that isn't possible. Some will survive because of what we did here today, but most will die. There is no stopping that now."

Kleito tore her eyes away from the sight, her ears filling with the screams in the streets. She turned to her team. "Return to your posts, our city will need us to maintain order."

"Yes, ma'am!" came some of the replies, but the avoided eye contact told her few would heed what might be her final order, instead running to spend their last few minutes of life with their loved ones. She didn't blame them, and she longed to have someone to share her final moments with as well. She looked at the old man.

"I should take you in."

"For what?"

"For harboring a fugitive."

He shrugged. "I wasn't aware he was one. And besides, even if you lock me up now, I'll never see the inside of a courtroom. Nothing will be left."

She stole a glance out the window, the sky rapidly darkening. "How long?"

Gadeiros frowned, shaking his head slowly. "I don't know. We have no experience with this. Days? Hours? Minutes? I don't know."

She turned to him. "If you knew, why didn't you save yourself?"

He chuckled, returning to the living area and retrieving his glass of wine, refilling it before taking a sip. "I'm too old to rebuild." He regarded her. "But you aren't. Why don't you join them?"

Her eyes narrowed, her heart hammering. "Who? The group you put together?"

"Yes, why not? You're young, strong, intelligent. You're exactly what a new Atlantis will need to rebuild."

The house shook again, and part of the ceiling collapsed. She lunged forward, throwing herself over the old man as debris rained down on them. It stopped, and she rose, dusting off. "Are you okay?"

He nodded, frowning at his dust-filled glass. "Yes, but I'm afraid my drink has been ruined." He tossed its contents against the wall, apparently no longer concerned about the cleanliness of his home, then refilled his glass. "I think I shall retire to the garden. There are fewer things to fall upon my head there." He made for the backyard, then stopped, turning back toward her. "If you choose to join them, then you must hurry. They're at Pier Six, at the farthest end of Canal Four."

She didn't reply, unsure of what to say. The screams outside were a mix of panic and anger, and she knew the city she loved was descending into anarchy as she stood here, debating an offer to escape it all. Part of her wanted to flee the destruction, but another part of her couldn't get past what her duty to her people meant. These were exactly the times people like her were needed, when law and order collapsed.

Suddenly the ground shook violently, tossing her off her feet, a terrifying howling sound filling her ears, as if a beast were emerging from under the ground.

And it nearly caused her to soil herself.

"What was that?" she cried as she picked herself up, rushing to help the old man who had collapsed in the next room, his glass miraculously saved.

"I have no idea," replied the visibly shaken man, his own eyes filled with the fear she shared.

"It sounded like some beast!"

The man headed for his courtyard, shaking his head. "Don't be a fool. There are no such beasts."

Her hammering heart and jittering limbs were threatening to overwhelm her, and she began to grow faint when she finally remembered to breathe. She sucked in a deep breath, the world coming back into focus before she was slammed with a thought that almost knocked her out.

"It's the gods!"

Gadeiros stopped and turned to face her. "What?"

Her eyes were wide now, her ears pounding as her thought turned into absolute certainty. "It has to be! The gods are angry, and they've come to take their revenge on us for tossing them aside. We were arrogant to think we could survive without them, and now they're back to deliver justice!"

Gadeiros frowned at her. "I see now I was mistaken in thinking you were intelligent."

She glared at him. "And you have a better explanation?" She jabbed the air between them with her finger. "Today Poseidon's Trident was not only desecrated, touched by a human for the first time in centuries, but it was stolen as well. And now, only hours later, the mountain erupts with fire, and our city shakes and our buildings collapse around us? You think that's only coincidence?"

The old man stared at her, then shook his head, grabbing another carafe of wine. "I'm getting drunk." He paused, frowning as he stared at her. "Don't let your fear control you. There's still a chance to save yourself."

She shook her head as she realized what she had to do. "No, Professor, I can save us all."

Zek Gerald Residence

Outside Beja, Portugal

Present Day

"Stay in the car."

Reading frowned at Chief Ventura, but nodded. This wasn't his jurisdiction, and his son was with him, and still technically a civilian. But staying here also meant he couldn't at least try to influence what was about to happen. The dozen men that now surrounded the house of one Zek Gerald, were clearly locals, and clearly had no idea what they were doing when it came to a hostage situation like this. As far as Reading's read of their intent went, they were planning on assaulting the house without any preamble.

He cursed as his suspicions were confirmed and the front door was kicked in without warning, half a dozen armed men entering the premises, shouting. A shot rang out, then half a dozen more. Reading turned to Spencer.

177

"Stay put."

He threw the door open and sprinted toward the entrance.

And his friends.

Acton's eyes bulged at the sound of someone breaking into the house, the pounding of multiple sets of heavy footwear suggesting at least several attackers. He couldn't understand a word they were saying, but something sounded like the word 'police' to him.

Zek and Tark rushed to the door, Tark with a weapon.

This is going to get ugly fast.

He tipped himself to the side, balancing all his weight on two of the chair legs. It took only a moment for them to snap, and he collapsed to the floor, the cheap wood splintering. He pulled with all his might, snapping his arms free, and stood, his wrists bleeding. He lifted Laura in her chair, carrying her behind the kitchen island before tipping her onto her side so her head wasn't in plain view as more shots erupted.

"Tark!"

The horror in Zek's voice suggested his brother had just been shot or worse, and Acton caught a glimpse of Spud sprinting past, toward the back of the house. Acton reached up and grabbed a steak knife from a knife block on the counter, and cut the ties binding Laura. She flipped over onto her hands and knees, crouching behind the island as footfalls stormed into the kitchen. Acton raised his hands, keeping the rest of his body out of sight.

"We're the hostages! Don't shoot!"

Laura's hands shot up beside him as men from either side of the island appeared, guns pointed at him then Laura, shouting uselessly in Portuguese.

"Bloody hell! They're the ones you're here to save!"

Acton breathed an audible sigh of relief at Reading's voice. Somebody snapped some orders and the guns were raised, their ordeal over.

Shots cracked the air in the rear of the house, making a liar out of him.

Spud pressed the phone against his ear, praying that Thatcher would pick up.

"Who is this?"

He recognized Tarrell Fleming's voice. He wasn't Thatcher, but he'd have to do, the footfalls getting closer. "It's me, Spud. We're under attack. The hostages are about to be rescued, and I think I'm going to die. Tell Thatcher that the prisoners know what we're doing. They know about the—"

Shots splintered the bathroom door, the lock shattering, and suddenly the door was kicked open, the top hinge failing. Spud thrust his hands into the air. "I surrender!"

Two weapons discharged, each firing a shot, then two then three. He shook from the blasts, the searing pain of each shot rapidly fading as the next overwhelmed him. His arms slumped to the floor, the still connected phone sliding onto the cheap linoleum.

And he asked God one last question.

Why? We were only trying to help save the world.

Acton sat on the rear bumper of the ambulance as his wrists were tended to. Laura stood nearby, hers red but the skin uncut, tears in her eyes as three bodies were pushed past them on gurneys. She shook her head at Reading, who acknowledged her, but signaled her with a look to say nothing as he spoke to the man apparently in charge of the fiasco. A handshake was exchanged, and Reading finally joined them.

"Will he be okay?"

The paramedic nodded. "Just have them looked at when you get back home. The dressings will need to be changed, and your doctor should monitor for infection."

Acton examined the tidy wrapping job. "Thanks. Good work." He stood and Laura gave him a hug. He returned it, then looked at Reading. "Can we go?"

"Yes, but they're going to want to interview you in the next day or so. They're asking for you to stay in Portugal until you do."

Acton lowered his voice. "So then going back to the Azores is permitted?"

Reading's eyes widened. "I suppose so. Why? You're not going back to those ruins, are you?"

"Of course I am, but curiosity isn't the reason."

Reading's eyes narrowed. "Explain."

"Don't you know why they kidnapped us?"

Reading shook his head. "Enlighten me."

"I spotted them planting a bomb."

Reading's eyes shot wide again. "What bomb?"

"These guys are some sort of do-gooder terrorist group that intends to blow up all the transatlantic data cables to send some sort of political message."

Reading cursed. "We need to get that info to the proper authorities immediately."

Acton nodded. "I agree, but these guys"—he threw a thumb over his shoulder at the local police responsible for an unnecessary massacre—"aren't them."

Reading pursed his lips. "Agreed. Let's get somewhere private so we can make the necessary calls."

"I suggest our plane. You can make all the calls you need, and we can get back to the Azores to try and stop whatever it is they're doing. If we don't, Atlantis could be lost to the world once again."

EQ Hotel & Casino
Shanghai, China

Kane dropped silently back onto his suite's balcony, his job done. The hotel's IT system had been tapped, the drives copied, and all evidence he had been upstairs removed. Now Langley just had to decrypt the data, and hopefully find the proof they needed that Zhang was behind the illegal weapons systems, and ideally, their location so they could be recovered or destroyed.

He stepped back inside his room, sliding the balcony door shut, then quickly stripped out of his black light absorbing infiltration suit, carefully wrapping it back up and putting it in the false bottom of his toiletries bag. Back in his skivvies, he climbed into his bed. "Status on my guest?"

"Still sound asleep on the couch," replied the familiar voice in his ear. He settled himself. "Am I good?"

"You're on your wrong side."

Kane frowned, flipping over and readjusting. "Good?"

"Perfect. Pull your underwear down a little."

He reached for the elastic band on instinct, then paused. "Wait a minute. Are you just trying to see my ass?"

"I'd never do a thing like that."

Kane raised his hand, giving the finger to the cameras now overridden by his team.

"Switching in three, two, one, switching."

Kane lowered his arms and closed his eyes as the countdown progressed, trying to be as relaxed as possible for his hosts when the feed was returned to their control. "Okay, you're back on the live feed. No evidence that they've noticed anything."

Kane's watch pulsed and he cursed to himself.

Perfect timing.

He gave himself a sixty count then stretched and yawned. He rolled out of bed then used the bathroom, pretending to squint at his watch, the display indicating another message from Reading. He gave an exaggerated yawn then grabbed his phone and a cigarette, heading again for the balcony's blind spot. He brought up Reading's encrypted message, his eyes shooting wide and his heart racing as he read the update.

Then immediately forwarded it to Leroux with an *Urgent* tag.

Operations Center 3, CIA Headquarters

Langley, Virginia

Leroux's terminal beeped with an urgent communication, and he returned to his desk, tapping at the keyboard, his eyes widening as he read Kane's message, then the details forwarded by Agent Reading. He rose. "Okay, people, new intel. Our two professors were just rescued by Portuguese authorities, and they are now safe."

A round of applause erupted, and shivers rushed over his body as he realized his team was just as committed to saving these people as he was, and just as relieved that being forced off the case hadn't resulted in innocent lives lost.

He held up his hand. "We'll have cake and drinks later to celebrate." Laughter. "Here's the critical tidbit. According to Agent Reading, the people who kidnapped our professors, are the *same* people we've been looking for. Apparently, they are the ones who set the charges on the data cables, and the professors stumbled upon them in the Azores." He turned to Child. "Please tell me you're still monitoring any communications from that ship."

Child tapped at his keyboard. "Yup. I figured you said *we* had to stop working on it, not the equipment."

Leroux smiled. "I knew there was a reason I wanted you on my team."

Child grinned. "I thought it was my rugged good looks."

Leroux gave him the eye. "You're not my type. What have you got?"

"I have a shore-to-ship call just a few minutes ago, originating in mainland Portugal."

Leroux nodded. "Probably our kidnappers phoning home. Anything else?"

Child shook his head then held up a finger. "Wait, someone's making a call right now. Why aren't they using satellite phones?"

"Maybe they're Luddites."

"Well, Luddites or not, that call is using some serious over-the-air encryption."

"Can you trace it?"

"Give me a second. The number they're calling isn't encrypted." Child furiously typed away, then suddenly shoved away from his keyboard, arms in the air, a smile on his face. "I can't track it the entire way, but guess where the number they're calling was routed through."

Leroux smiled. "The same Russian civilian satellite our blackmailer used?"

Child smiled. "It's like you don't even need me."

Leroux chuckled. "Well, if I'm asked to make cuts, I'll know where to start." The room erupted with laughter at Child's expense. He spun in his chair, hand held high, flipping them the bird. "Okay, so we've got two communications, both from the same organization, both using the same Russian civilian satellite, a satellite we've confirmed is often used by the Russian government, including military, when necessary. I think this confirms that the use of this satellite isn't a fluke." He turned to Tong. "Did you ever get a response back on the tail numbers for the two planes?"

She checked her terminal. "Yes, it just came in. Confirmed Russian Air Force, based out of Chkalovsky Airbase just outside Moscow."

Child laughed. "Well, you're never going to guess where our signal was routed to."

Leroux turned back toward Child. "Chkalovsky?"

"Yup. I can't track it past there, but that ship-to-shore call that they're making right now, is being carried over an encrypted carrier wave to mainland Portugal, then bounced up to a specific Russian civilian satellite, which then routed it to its end destination at Chkalovsky. From there it's probably being routed directly to those planes using Russian Air Force equipment."

Leroux turned to stare at the footage still being fed them from the aircraft monitoring the strangely behaving Russian. "I think you're absolutely right. And that means the Russians *are* involved."

East of the Azores, Atlantic Ocean

Thatcher stared at the radio, unsure of what to make of the conversation he had just had. There was still a technical problem with the satellite, which he found odd, but in discussing it with the others, they had all agreed it was possible, though none could believe it would be down for as long as it was.

Yet when challenged, their benefactor had erupted with rage, insulting him and his family, and pretty much anyone he had ever known, before it devolved further into what he assumed was Russian. "Wait a minute. How did you call me?"

"I couldn't get through on the satellite system."

"I know, I'm blocking you. So how did you call me?"

"I used the ship-to-shore system. It's encrypted."

"But what number?"

"I called your cellphone. I figured you'd have it routed to wherever you are."

More curses erupted then the signal went dead, with no instructions as to what to do.

If the man was lying, there was nothing he could do about it. Kozhin had control of all the detonators. He didn't even have access to the ones his team had set. If he did want to set one of the charges off, he'd have to dive back down to where they laid the charge, and manually detonate it, killing himself.

Yet if Kozhin were telling the truth, then all he had to be was patient. Eventually, the satellite would be out of maintenance mode, and the detonation signals would be sent, along with the message he and the others had crafted for months. He sighed as he leaned back in his chair.

Please God, let him not be lying.

But what reason could the man have for lying? The charges were laid, *that* he knew. Blowing the cables was the only thing that those charges could be used for. There was only one reason to do that, and that was to send a message to the masses.

The blood drained from his face and he felt woozy as another possibility occurred to him.

Blackmail!

The detonation of the charges would cause billions in damage and disruption. Would governments pay to prevent it? Would corporations?

How well do you know this man?

He didn't really know him at all. He had been enamored with the money and the possibilities it brought, and he had never questioned where the money was coming from. The man was Russian, which should have raised some flags, but he was of the opinion that people should be judged individually, rather than collectively.

You're too trusting.

It was something his mother had always told him, and perhaps she was right. It meant people taking advantage of him all his life, despite the fact he considered himself intelligent. He always wanted to think the best of people, but far too often, humanity was revealed to be the cesspool it was.

Could Kozhin be using his plan for profit?

He suddenly felt sick to his stomach.

What do I tell the others?

He doubled over, battling the desire to vomit.

Nothing!

He couldn't tell them. Everyone's spirits were still high despite the delay, and regardless of whether he was right or wrong, there was nothing they could do about it.

You'll just have to wait and hope.

He rushed from the radio room and bent over the railing, the battle lost.

Departing Beja, Portugal

Acton breathed a sigh of relief the moment the wheels of the Gulf V left the runway, then the frustrations he had kept bottled up erupted. "What the hell was that?"

Reading, sitting across from them with his son, shook his head, frowning. "That was the most inept rescue I've ever been part of."

Acton regarded the young Spencer and frowned, the boy appearing pale and withdrawn. "Are you okay?"

Spencer seemed surprised at being spoken to. "Umm, yeah, I guess."

Reading turned in his seat to face his son a little better. "*That* was not the way things are supposed to go down in those situations. You'll be trained on how to deal with these things, and I'm sorry to say, you'll eventually get used to seeing bodies, though it'll be rare that you see them like that. That was a disgusting example of amateurs trying to be heroes. There was no reason to not negotiate for the hostages. Nobody had to die there." He sighed, lowering his voice. "I'm sorry you saw that. I shouldn't have brought you."

Spencer's eyes widened and he stared at his father, shaking his head. "It's not your fault, and I'm glad you did." He paused, as if searching for words. "Look, I've known I've wanted to be a copper for a while, now. This just makes me want to be one even more. I want to learn how to do things right, so that if I'm ever in a situation like today, I'll know the proper thing to do. If you were running that operation, none of that would have happened, and everyone would be alive. I want to learn to do it like you."

Acton watched as Reading struggled to maintain control. His friend was bursting with pride that his humility was struggling to suppress, all while he took in what was probably the nicest thing his son had ever said to him since the end of their estrangement. Acton reached over and squeezed Laura's hand.

Three times.

I. Love. You.

She returned the gesture with a smile as they both enjoyed the moment. Acton decided to save his friend from embarrassing himself. He held up his wrists.

"We must have a first aid kit on board."

Laura nodded. "I'm sure we do, but those bandages are fresh. We should just leave them."

He agreed. "Let's just keep it in mind for when we're done with all this."

"Do they hurt?"

"Are you the most beautiful woman in the world?"

She gave him the eye. "So that's a no."

Spencer snickered and Reading groaned, their awkward moment broken, Acton's job done. He patted Laura's cheek. "So beautiful yet so modest." He slowly rotated both wrists and winced. "Yeah, they hurt, but nothing I can't live with."

Reading frowned. "If you intend to jump into the water and disarm a bomb—something, I remind you, you have no clue how to do—then not only are you going to be crying like a baby from the salt water on those wounds, you're going to be attracting every damned shark in the area."

Acton regarded his friend. "Who invited the voice of reason?"

"He invited himself when he saved your arses."

Acton rolled his eyes and winked at Laura. "Something tells me we'll never hear the end of that." He became serious, holding up one of his bandaged limbs. "You're right, of course. We can't go in the water, not with a bomb there. But if we get there in time, hopefully we can direct the authorities to where the bomb is. Have you been able to reach anyone?"

Reading tapped the phone sitting on his crossed leg. "I've sent a message to Dylan, and my partner back in London will be working with the Portuguese authorities. Hopefully by the time we get there, this will all be over."

Acton checked his watch. "Well, I've told the pilot to push it, so we'll be there in less than an hour and a half."

Laura leaned closer to him. "Mary is arranging for a vehicle to be waiting for us, and for dive equipment to be ready, just in case we do decide to go in."

Reading stabbed the air between them with a finger. "*Not* going to happen."

"Well, let's just hope the Portuguese get there in time, with the proper expertise. I don't give a damn about that cable, but if it detonates, it could send the entire find sliding down even farther."

Reading frowned. "What would that mean?"

Acton shrugged. "It depends on how bad it is. It's already pretty close to the maximum depth we can dive in suits, without having to switch to hydrox or something. If it slides too far, then only submersibles will be able to reach it, but that's only if it's exposed. If it slides and gets buried again, we might not ever find it. Nobody is going to be able to afford a dig that deep without an exact location. It could be years, even decades, before anybody could make an attempt."

Laura squeezed his hand. "Let's pray that doesn't happen."

Director Morrison's Office, CIA Headquarters

Langley, Virginia

National Clandestine Service Chief Leif Morrison looked up from his computer and pointed at one of his chairs as Leroux entered. Little progress had been made so far, except that the French authorities had confirmed the cable had been severed physically, and likely by an explosive. Other cables were being inspected, but it would take time to get teams in place, and it couldn't be rushed, since no one knew which was due to be detonated in only minutes, their time almost up.

"You said it was urgent."

Leroux nodded, dropping in the chair. "Yes, sir. It's about the professors."

Morrison frowned. "I thought I told you to drop it."

Leroux paled slightly. "We did! We passed everything to Dylan and Agent Reading, then left it. But I just received an urgent communique from Dylan. The professors have been rescued, and they said that their kidnappers claimed to be the ones who planted the explosives on the cables."

Morrison's eyebrows rose. "You're kidding me."

Leroux shook his head. "No, sir."

Morrison leaned forward. "I sense you've found out something."

"Yes, sir. During the rescue, a call was made from the location of the hostage rescue, to the boat we had been monitoring that we thought might be involved in their kidnapping. A boat that had some serious dive equipment on board."

"To plant the explosives."

"That's our working theory. Anyway, just minutes ago, a ship-to-shore call was placed from the boat. It used some serious encryption, so we weren't able to monitor what was said, but the landline it connected to in mainland Portugal, routed the call through the same Russian satellite that our extortionist used."

A smile slowly crept up the side of Morrison's face. "Coincidence?"

Leroux's smile grew to match. "No, I don't think so. We were able to trace the routing to Chkalovsky Airbase near Moscow, the same place the two Russian planes are based."

"What planes?"

"Oh, sorry, I never mentioned it because we hadn't connected them until just now. A Russian Ilyushin Il-80 been circling over the Atlantic for hours, been refueled at least once already, and another tanker is on its way. Some assets were scrambled to monitor, since it was behaving oddly, and there's been no communication with them except to basically tell our guys to back off."

"So you're thinking what?"

"I'm thinking that it's too big a coincidence that these Russian military jets are based in the same location our blackmailers just placed a call to."

Morrison leaned back. "My God, Chris, are you saying that the Russians are behind this after all?"

Leroux shrugged. "I find it hard to believe they couldn't be, if these planes are Russian military."

Morrison sighed heavily. The idea that the Russians could actually be behind this was unthinkable. What they would have to gain, beyond simply causing havoc from behind their wall of nuclear missiles, was beyond him. But the nation was so corrupt, there was another possibility. "A rogue element."

Leroux nodded. "That's what I'm hoping, but either way, there's not much we can do. The next detonation is in minutes. Without blowing that plane out of the sky, there's no way to know for sure."

"*That's* out of the question."

Leroux frowned. "I know. But I do have an idea on how we can confirm things."

Morrison's eyebrows rose. "Oh?"

"Let them detonate the next cable."

National Defense Management Center

Moscow, Russian Federation

"Petra, I'm calling as a friend, not a representative of the American government."

Major Petra Yolkin frowned as she stared at the phone. She hadn't heard from the man on the other end of the line in years—in over a decade. But she had followed his career, and knew he had made something of himself, and his reputation was still that of an honest man. And everything he had told her was so fantastical, he had either had a mental break, or he was telling the truth. She was leaning toward the latter. "If this is true, why haven't we heard anything?"

"It's all very hush-hush on this end. We think we've tracked them, but I need your help."

"You're asking a lot, Leif."

"I know, but have I ever lied to you?"

She laughed. "It's been at least ten years. There hasn't exactly been a lot of opportunity." She could almost hear him smile through the phone.

"Trust me on this. Find out about those planes. If they're legitimately there, we need to know, because in a few minutes, we could be blowing them out of the sky, and that could start a war."

Yolkin frowned as she stared at her screen, part of Morrison's story already confirmed. The tail numbers were legitimate, and they were based at Chkalovsky Airbase. Now the question was why they were over the middle of the Atlantic, one of them going in circles, the other about to refuel it. "I'll get back to you."

"Make it quick. We're out of time."

Conference Room 212, CIA Headquarters

Langley, Virginia

"One dollar? Are you insane?"

Morrison shrugged at White House Chief of Staff Nelson. "Quite possibly, but our psych profile suggests this will infuriate him, and force him to call us live, as opposed to sending a pre-recorded message."

"It's liable to infuriate him and push him to detonate everything."

"Possibly, but we don't think so. The President still has no intention of paying him?"

"No, he's committed to that course."

"Then the next detonation is in less than two minutes. We need to send our message now."

There was a pause, then Nelson nodded. "Do it."

Another talking head spoke a moment later. "Done. Exactly one dollar has been transferred to the account."

"When will they know?"

Morrison leaned forward. "My bet is he already does."

Somewhere over the Atlantic

Konstantin Kozhin glared at the display. One dollar? Was it a mistake? He refreshed the page, and again the same digits appeared. *1.00 USD.* "Who the hell do they think they're dealing with?"

He growled at the empty cabin as he glanced out the window, something catching his eye. One of the American fighter jets had broken away, followed by the others.

Maybe they've lost interest.

He wasn't worried about them. They were in a Russian registered aircraft, and the Americans wouldn't dare touch them. He hadn't planned on being found, especially before the mission was accomplished, but they had contingencies in place. Their refueling aircraft would be here again soon, then they'd have another six hours in the air, and could be refueled as many times as necessary. If the Americans hadn't backed off by then, they'd simply fly back to Russia, ending any pursuit, and the dirt he had on General Gorokhin would ensure their safe arrival and escape.

With what looked like two billion dollars, rather than one.

One dollar.

They're not taking me seriously.

He brought up the detonator control interface, selecting another cable, this time off the coast of Spain, then had the computer dial the White House.

Time for a personal chat with the President.

Conference Room 212, CIA Headquarters

Langley, Virginia

"It's him."

Leroux's heart pounded, sweat beading on his back and running down his spine. This was *his* plan, and if it didn't work, he'd wear it. What that meant, he wasn't sure, but it couldn't be good. Everything had to proceed like clockwork, and everyone had to react the way he had predicted. They had sent the single dollar, and now they had a call. The question was whether it was a live call.

"You seem to think I'm joking, Mr. President."

Leroux and Morrison exchanged grins.

"This is White House Chief of Staff Nelson, speaking on behalf of the President. We do not think you are joking, sir, but we need more time."

The silhouette displayed leaned closer to the camera as the Chairman of the Joint Chiefs of Staff whispered into his phone. "Nonsense. You've just lost another data cable, and the price has gone up to two billion dollars."

Somewhere over the Atlantic

"Echo Leader, this is ParkRanger, proceed, over."

USAF Major Chariya "Apocalypta" Em dropped back from the left wing of the Russian, wishing she knew what the hell was going on. She had never been ordered to buzz a Russian aircraft before, and didn't know anyone who had done it at Mach speeds. Then again, she had never been stationed in this area before, so maybe this was more common here.

Bullshit.

"Okay guys, everyone back off, just in case our friends overreact." She watched the rest of her flight break away, the Il-80 still in a slow counterclockwise turn, the refueling aircraft now only minutes away. She checked her range and said a silent prayer. "Here goes nothing."

She pushed forward on her throttle, the acceleration shoving her into her seat as the g-forces rapidly increased. Normally these speeds would be a thrill, but precision flying while accelerating was an art, and buzzing an aircraft traveling at dramatically slower speeds, while it was banking, required mathematical precision, not broad brush strokes. She rapidly closed the distance on the Russian, not bothering to check her airspeed indicator—her orders were to pass as closely and loudly as possible, nothing more.

The Russian was slowly banking into her path. Approaching from the other side would be useless, as she'd end up too far away for what she assumed would be the desired effect—a reaction from the pilot.

Too late to change my mind.

Instinct told her to close her eyes, training told her to keep the damned things open. She squinted instead, bracing for a screw-up, then blasted past, banking left to display her weapons pods and give them a taste of her exhaust, mere feet from the cockpit.

"There they go!" cried one of her wingmen, and she eased off the throttle, continuing to turn, her head twisted back so she could see what was going on. She smiled as the Russian came back into view, now banking in the opposite direction.

"Now that was precision flying!"

She laughed, and activated her comm, trying to keep the excitement out of her voice. "ParkRanger, Echo Flight Leader. Mission accomplished, over."

Kozhin gripped the desk as the plane banked hard to the right, its engines whining, his ears still recovering from the screaming sound of moments ago. He continued to stare at the camera, straightening himself, the Americans outside apparently playing games. The question was whether the left hand knew what the right was doing, and since these shadows had been here long before he detonated the first cable, he had to assume they weren't related.

"You have two hours, then I detonate another cable, and the price goes to four billion. Don't trifle with me, gentlemen. You still have time to get out of the mess you've made."

He ended the call, then stormed out of his cabin and toward the cockpit. "What the hell just happened?"

The pilot glanced over his shoulder. "The bastards buzzed us. He missed us by less than ten meters!"

"Could they know?"

"Bah! It's the same assholes who've been here the entire time. Those stupid Americans know nothing."

Kozhin frowned, not entirely sure whether to agree with the man or not. "Perhaps we should head back, just in case."

"Let's get refueled first. If they interfere with that, we won't have too many options."

"How much fuel do we have?"

"Just enough to get us to America, or Mother Russia over the polar route. But if we don't refuel soon, it's Europe, Iceland, or Greenland."

"Or the drink," added the copilot.

Kozhin frowned. "Let's refuel then head back to base. Can we still detonate the bombs?"

"We'll be able to for a couple of hours, then we'd need to bounce the signal through another satellite."

Kozhin nodded. "Well, if they don't pay us in the next two hours, they probably never will, so we'll just detonate them all anyway."

Conference Room 212, CIA Headquarters
Langley, Virginia

Morrison slapped Leroux on the back as handshakes were exchanged around the room. "Well, that pretty much confirms it," Morrison said as the clip replayed on a loop, their subject clearly leaning into an unexpected movement, the scream of jet engines audible in the background. Their mystery man was definitely on the plane, and Leroux was the hero of the moment with people he barely knew shaking his hand.

"So, what do we do now?" someone asked, the room settling down.

Morrison looked at the faces surrounding them. "I say we let the Russians handle them."

Chief of Staff Nelsen nodded slowly. "And if they don't?"

"Then we blow him out of the sky before the deadline."

Nods of agreement rounded the room and the displays as Leroux's phone vibrated with a message. He pulled it out of his pocket and read the urgent message from Child, then cursed.

Out loud.

Morrison turned toward him. "What is it?"

Leroux blushed. "Sorry for that. Umm, we've got a problem."

"What?"

"The media has the story. Apparently, the explosion of the second data cable was caught by a news crew that happened to be filming in the area. CNN just picked it up."

Curses filled the room.

Approaching Chkalovsky Airbase, Russian Federation

Major Petra Yolkin sat in the Mil Mi-17 transport helicopter, trying to remain as calm as possible, at least to the men surrounding her. It was tough being a woman in her position, especially at this moment. These men were the best of the best. Battle-hardened Special Forces—Spetsnaz. They were the best at what they did, and in every Russian's opinion, better than anything the Americans had to offer.

She wasn't so sure that they were better, but perhaps they were more effective. It helped when your rules of engagement were essentially kill everything in sight. Americans and their Western counterparts were too concerned about minimizing civilian casualties. Russians had no qualms about killing anyone who got in the way.

And today, she had a feeling the bodies were going to pile up, though thankfully, where they were heading had no civilians, or at least very few.

She had confirmed that the planes Morrison had identified were Russian, she had confirmed that they were supposed to be at Chkalovsky, and she confirmed that they were definitely not supposed to be over the Atlantic Ocean. She hadn't bothered calling the base to find out—that would only tip them off.

When she had taken what she found to her superior, he had been incensed, and within minutes, she was in the rear of one of two choppers, with a team of forty, heading for the base. Her orders: shut down whatever General Gorokhin was up to. With tensions high around the world with respect to Russia, Moscow didn't want to risk further enflaming them by getting mixed up in a conspiracy to blackmail the American government.

"Two minutes!" called the pilot, and the team began an equipment check, the major in charge leaning closer.

"Stay behind us, and don't hesitate to use that." He pointed at her sidearm. "Assume everyone is involved."

She nodded, her heart hammering at the idea. This was a military base. Heavily armed. They'd be outnumbered perhaps hundreds-to-one. But they were assaulting a single building where the General was confirmed to be currently on a conference call with Moscow, and that building would be mostly administrative staff. By the time the rest of the base reacted, it should be over.

If everything went to plan.

If.

She spotted the base ahead, the runways visible now, the sprawling complex stretched out beyond.

This is it.

The chopper's nose dipped as it gained speed, the ground streaking by, before it suddenly pulled up then dropped rapidly toward the ground. She gripped her seat as the doors opened, the Spetsnaz team leaping out either side before they even landed. She jumped out a few moments after them, the massive helicopter rising immediately behind her as she took a few deep breaths, gaining her bearings as the second chopper lifted off. The forty-strong team of elite soldiers was already rushing ahead in a wedge formation, the only base personnel visible either not noticing, or standing with their mouths agape, wondering what was going on.

The headquarters building with General Gorokhin lay ahead of them. Two guards at the top of the steps advanced, their weapons raised. They were taken out with suppressed weapons.

But nothing prevented the eyes of those around them from seeing what had just happened.

Shouts of anger and panic surrounded them as they reached the steps, then a siren blared. Gunfire from their left erupted, tearing at the façade of the building.

But the team didn't stop.

The threat from the lone weapon would end the moment they crossed the threshold. She ducked, not there yet, and not used to shots being fired at her. More gunfire inside had her slowing down, but one of her team grabbed her by the arm and hauled her along with him, the heavy doors slamming shut behind them. Bursts of gunfire echoed around her, and she realized her eyes were closed. She forced them

213

open, and gasped at the lobby littered with bodies, soldiers, and administrative staff, dead or dying around her.

A dozen men were left to guard the lobby, and she spotted the rest of the team rushing the stairs to her right. She sprinted after them as the gunfire continued on the next floor that housed the senior staff including the general. She made it to the first landing, two more bodies staring up at her, all life drained from their eyes, as shouts and screams continued.

She made it to a sitting area at the top of the stairs, several dead in the comfortable leather couches, her stomach flipping as she recognized General Osinov, a man she had tremendous respect for, and who certainly had nothing to do with what was happening.

We need him alive!

She raced after the still advancing team, the General's office at the end of the long hallway. His door was closed, and as the team efficiently cleared the rooms before they passed, each receiving a burst of gunfire, she caught up to the major as he reached the General's door. He booted it open and she pushed past him, slapping the barrel of his Kashkan submachine gun toward the floor. She drew her own weapon and aimed it at the General's head as he rose from his desk, the phone still pressed against his ear.

"What is the meaning of this? Who are you?"

"I am Major Petra Yolkin, Military Police. General Gorokhin, you are under arrest for the illegal use of property belonging to the Russian people, and for a hell of a lot more before this day is out."

214

The phone was returned to its cradle as the color drained from the General's face. "I have no idea what you're talking about."

"The planes, General." She pulled out her phone, bringing up the record. "One Ilyushin Il-80, tail number RA-86147, and one Ilyushin Il-78 aerial refueling tanker, tail number CCCP-78823. Where are these planes, General?"

A deep breath was drawn from behind the desk, some color returning. "They are on exercise over the Atlantic."

"That exercise was not approved by Moscow, General."

He glared at her. "Since when do I need permission from Moscow to train my own people?"

"I'm the one asking the questions, General. Who is on that plane?"

"What?"

"Who is on the plane, circling in the Atlantic for no apparent reason, being regularly refueled from this base?"

"I have no idea what you're talking about."

The major stepped forward. "May I?"

She nodded, and the Spetsnaz commander put a bullet in the General's leg. He screamed out in pain and collapsed to his knees as he struggled to hold himself up with the desk. She stepped closer.

"General, you have another leg, and my orders give me a lot of leeway. I'll ask you again. *Who* is on the plane?"

The General gave up, grasping his leg as he tried to stem the pain and blood. "H-his name is Konstantin Kozhin."

Yolkin exchanged a glance with the major, who shrugged. "Who is Konstantin Kozhin?"

"The son of someone from my past. He threatened to reveal some family secrets if I didn't cooperate."

"What family secrets?"

Gorokhin glared at her through the pain. "If I told you, then that would defeat the purpose of me having betrayed my country, now wouldn't it!"

The major raised his weapon.

"Go ahead, shoot me, I'm dead anyway."

Yolkin raised her hand, waving the major off, just in case he decided to take Gorokhin up on his suggestion. "What did he want?"

"The Il-80 with tankers for twenty-four hours."

"And what did you get in return?"

"Fifty million American dollars, and a promise to never be bothered again."

"And why did he need the planes?"

Gorokhin shrugged. "I have no idea."

Yolkin shook her head, disgusted with the pathetic creature on his knees in front of her. She pulled out her phone and dialed Morrison first, just in case her superiors gave her orders preventing her from doing so.

"Morrison."

"It's me. His name is Konstantin Kozhin."

"What are you going to do?"

"My guess is take them down."

"Take out the tanker. Leave the other one."

"Are you sure?"

"He's the key to shutting down their network. We need him alive."

"I'll see what I can do."

"Thanks, I owe you one."

The call ended, and she dialed Moscow. "It's been confirmed. He gave the planes to a man named Konstantin Kozhin. He says he doesn't know why, but we do."

"Who's manning the planes?"

She chastised herself for not thinking to ask the question. She pressed the phone against her chest. "Who's manning the planes?"

Gorokhin stared up at her, his face filled with pain. "What?"

"The crew! Are they ours, or his?"

"H-his. From Medved Corps."

She cursed and nearly spit at the mention of the mercenaries made up of mostly men like those that now filled the room. She returned to her call. "Not our people."

"Then that settles that."

"Wait, the Americans want the Il-80 left alone. They want him alive."

There was a pause, and she tensed.

"You spoke to them?"

"I felt it was the diplomatic thing to do, since they were the ones who tipped us off."

Another pause. "Next time leave the diplomacy to me, Major."

She paled slightly. "Yes, sir."

"Is the Spetsnaz commander with you?"

"Yes, sir."

"Put him on."

She held out the phone. "He wants to talk to you."

The major took the phone and pressed it to his ear. "Yes?" He nodded. "Yes." He raised his weapon and emptied the magazine into the general, then handed the phone back to Yolkin. She snapped her jaw shut but there was nothing she could do about her wide-open eyes. She put the phone to her ear.

"Sir?" There was no response. She checked the display and found the call had been ended.

Along with her investigation.

East of the Azores, Atlantic Ocean

Thatcher had confined himself to his quarters after losing his lunch, feigning sleep whenever someone would check on him. Giselle had spotted his display, and word had evidently spread among those on board that he was sick, so the check-ins were merely out of concern for him, not the mission. Though the fact he had heard nothing, told him that the delay continued, and his suspicions continued to grow, along with his frustrations at being powerless to do anything about it.

There was a rap on the door and the hatch opened. "Thatch, are you awake?"

He faked a groan at Giselle's disturbance.

"Sorry, buddy, but you have to see this."

The urgency in her voice had him kicking his blanket aside and rolling upright in his bunk. "What is it?"

"I, ahh, don't know. You better see for yourself."

219

He rose, feigning a good stretch and yawn to make it at least appear he had been sleeping, then slowly followed her onto the deck. She urged him forward, and he found himself increasing his pace to keep up, something serious obviously occurring, continuing to cover up his secret doubts no longer of any importance. He entered the mess hall to find everyone gathered around the television.

"What's this?"

Giselle pointed at the television tuned to CNN. "They're saying that someone has detonated two of the transatlantic cables, and is demanding two billion dollars or they'll blow up more!"

Thatcher's jaw dropped as he edged closer to the screen, listening to the report, and watching video of an underwater explosion breaking the surface off the coast of Spain. It was a charge they had set themselves earlier in the week. He dropped into a chair. "What does this mean?"

Giselle grabbed him by the shoulder, staring down at him. "Don't you get it? He lied to us! He used us! This was his plan all along! Get us to plant the charges so if we were caught, we'd be blamed, then demand cash in exchange for not detonating them. He was never one of us!"

Everyone was staring at him now, anger and confusion on their faces, some with tear-stained cheeks. And he didn't blame them. They had been betrayed. There was no doubt now. And it was his fault. It had never occurred to him not to trust Kozhin. His excitement over finally doing something that might make a difference had clouded his judgment, and now all their hard work was about to pay off for a man who was no more than a criminal. No message would be sent to better mankind, no awareness raised to the dangers of social media. It would have all been a complete waste of time and effort.

Though not for their so-called benefactor.

He stood to make billions in ransom if whoever he was blackmailing gave in. The details seemed sketchy from what he was hearing. The first inkling the press had was the explosion, which was then linked to a cable that had been severed exactly two hours earlier. It was too much of a coincidence for the press not to pursue, and someone within the American administration had revealed the truth.

But was it the *complete* truth?

He rose, anger replacing the shock of betrayal.

"Do you know what's going on?" asked Giselle, still gripping his shoulder.

He shook his head. "No, but I'm going to find out."

Somewhere over the Atlantic

"Echo Flight Leader, ParkRanger. We have four new bogies entering your airspace, heading two-nine-zero. We believe they're Russian Sukhoi Su-33 fighters from the aircraft carrier Admiral Kuznetsov. Their intent is unknown. Give them a wide berth, over."

Apocalypta checked her instruments, the four new targets just coming into view. The tanker was less than a mile from rendezvousing with the Il-80, and her own flight was due for replacement shortly as their fuel was running low. When they had been deployed, it was to check out a curiosity. They would have left long ago, but something else was going on, and she had no clue what it was.

We don't exactly have CNN or Google up here.

If she needed to know, command would inform her—after all, she was responsible for six airframes and half a dozen pilots including herself. Keeping her in the dark could put all of them at risk. The fact she hadn't been informed, meant she had to trust she didn't need to know.

But four Sukhois, dispatched into the middle of the Atlantic from a Russian carrier? Those things were almost never in the Atlantic, which probably meant it was in transit from the Baltic to the Mediterranean, or farther. Her initial thoughts were that the Russians were pissed because she had buzzed their plane, but now she wasn't sure. If the Russians were pissed, she wouldn't have been ordered to just give them some space. Giving them space meant their focus was the same plane they had been watching. If the Russians were a threat, she would have been ordered to bug out, or prepare to engage.

The very idea had her heart hammering. The only time she had ever engaged something in the air was over Georgia, and it had been Russians then, as well.

I seem to attract them.

She had been the talk of the Air Force, despite what had happened being declared top secret. A lot of smiles and back slaps had been sent her way, without anything said. She was a hero, though she was careful not to let it get to her head. About all she took away from the event was that she now knew she could pull the trigger when necessary. She had always wondered.

Her lady balls were big.

"Okay everyone, let's back off and give our Russian friends some space to do whatever the hell it is they're here for." She banked left, away from the plane they had been shadowing, the rest of her flight breaking away with her as she made a slow loop that would bring her parallel to the new arrivals, but heading in the opposite direction with a wide enough berth that they wouldn't perceive her as a threat. Her system started beeping and flashing at her, indicating weapons systems on the incoming birds were active.

Okay, Rooskies, who's your target?

East of the Azores, Atlantic Ocean

"What the hell is going on? I just saw a report on CNN that you've detonated two of the bombs, and that you're demanding two billion dollars to not detonate the rest!"

Thatcher felt the heat radiating from his flushed face, his hammering heart pounding so hard he swore he felt it in his bones. He had to calm himself.

"Has the story broken?"

He glared at the radio, unsure of how to respond, the voice of their benefactor almost bemused. "So it's true? You've detonated two of the devices, two hours apart?"

"Yes."

"You told me there was a problem with the satellite."

"I lied."

A wave of weakness flowed through Thatcher. He gripped the edge of the table holding the communications equipment, and drew in several large, deep breaths. A hand on his shoulder caused him to flinch, and he looked up to see Giselle standing behind him, the anger in her eyes not directed at him, but at the speaker. "What is going on? I at least deserve the truth."

"The truth is that you are a naïve dreamer that was taken advantage of. You had an intriguing idea that I recognized could be used to my benefit. You provided the manpower and the patsies should something go wrong, and I provided the money and connections to actually execute a modified version of your plan."

Thatcher's eyes burned, tears threatening to escape their confines. "But the message! What about the message?"

Laughter erupted from the speaker. "The message was never going to be sent. It was useless. Even if you destroyed all the cables, they would be repaired in time, the data rerouted in the meantime, and in the end, nothing would have been accomplished. People don't care anymore. They want their social media, they want their fake friends. It's easier than real life. At least this way I'll get a little richer, and if you want, I'll even share some of it with your people. How's a million each sound?"

Giselle's hand tightened on his shoulder. He looked up at her and she shook her head, her jaw squared. He patted her hand. "You can take your money and shove it."

More laughter. "How did I know you were going to say that? Thatcher, I respect you. You're a man of principles, no matter how naïve they may be. I'm still going—wait a minute." Muffled voices could be heard, and Thatcher and Giselle exchanged concerned glances. "Are you sure? Then get us closer to the Americans!"

There was a squelch then nothing.

Thatcher stood, putting an arm around Giselle.

"What the hell was that?"

Thatcher shook his head. "I don't know, but hopefully it's karma coming to bite him on the ass."

"What are we going to do?"

Thatcher frowned. "The only thing we can do."

Somewhere over the Atlantic

Kozhin rushed toward the cockpit as the plane banked hard to the left, Anokhin, the former major in charge of the Medved Corps mercenaries he was employing, hot on his heels. He yanked open the cockpit door and pushed inside, the pilot and copilot shouting at each other as they pushed the Il-80 to its limits.

"What's going on?"

The pilot ignored him, leaving the copilot to answer. "Four tangoes are closing on our position. They've ordered us to return to Russia. General Gorokhin is dead."

Kozhin frowned.

That's disappointing.

He couldn't care less that Gorokhin was dead. The man was a corrupt bastard, but he had served a purpose, a purpose that he unfortunately still needed served. He turned to Anokhin. "What's your recommendation?"

"Obey their orders until we can execute the contingency plan."

Kozhin closed his eyes, tossing his head back as he gripped the doorframe, the plane finally leveling out. The contingency plan was insanity, and it had never occurred to him that they might actually need it. If he had, he never would have agreed to it, and demanded another plan.

But now, here they were, stuck.

"There they are!"

The pilot pointed slightly to their left and Kozhin stepped closer, peering out the cockpit window as four dots screamed toward them, the refueling aircraft banking away. Kozhin slammed his fist into the back of the copilot's seat.

"Shit! How are we for fuel?"

The copilot checked the gauge and shook his head. "If we want to get back to Russia, we have to leave now."

Suddenly the pilot cursed, and all their jaws dropped.

Apocalypta watched in shock and awe as a missile streaked from the weapons pod of the lead Sukhoi, the air-to-air weapon leaving a trail of spent fuel behind as it rapidly closed in on its target. She activated her comm as she watched the tanker bank away from the incoming missile, chaff erupting from its defense pods as it tried to escape the incoming certainty of death.

And it worked.

The missile veered left, slamming into the false heat signature and exploding, the shockwave pulsing through the air in all directions. But the reprieve was short-lived, two more missiles already tearing across the crisp blue sky.

"Let's back off some more. We don't want any of those missiles getting confused and locking on to us." She slowly banked away, doubling the distance, before leveling out so she could watch the show, the tanker continuing to turn, continuing to deploy chaff, when suddenly the decoys stopped.

They must be out.

Two missiles closed the gap, the massive tanker helpless, and Apocalypta silently said a prayer for its crew, whoever they were, as the missiles slammed into the fuselage. It erupted into a massive fireball, larger than anything she had ever seen, the 300,000 pounds of fuel on board putting on a display that would rival anything Hollywood could imagine.

"They're bugging out!"

Apocalypta checked her scope to confirm what she had just heard, then turned to see if she had missed the destruction of the focus of their attention.

It was still there.

I wonder why they left them alive.

Conference Room 212, CIA Headquarters
Langley, Virginia

Leroux sat in the briefing room, watching the video feeds from the assets monitoring the Russian attack, the wreckage of the tanker still collapsing toward the Atlantic far below. The Russians hadn't kept their word—they hadn't given any. But they had heeded the request to leave the plane carrying Konstantin Kozhin untouched.

They'd get it back eventually.

Perhaps.

It now all depended upon what Kozhin would do. He had limited options. His fuel would be getting low, so he'd have to make a decision soon. The Pentagon was estimating that he had barely enough fuel left to return to Russian territory if he took a polar route. But Leroux had a hunch that wasn't his plan, and probably never was. Returning to Russia would mean certain imprisonment, perhaps even an "accidental" death, since the Russians now knew what was going on, and when this was all over, and things were made public, the use of their military assets would result in embarrassment for the Kremlin. Perhaps if Kozhin had never been discovered, things might be different, but he still had a feeling Kozhin had never intended on setting foot on Russian soil—it was too dangerous.

He had his suspicions, and had voiced them to Morrison, though there was no way to confirm them until it was too late. Though there was one way it wouldn't matter, but they needed to force Kozhin into the only decision that could nullify any contingency plan he might have.

"We're ready, Mr. President."

Leroux snapped out of his reverie, staring at the screens at the front of the room, President Starling adjusting his tie.

"Make the call."

Somewhere over the Atlantic

"They're leaving!"

Kozhin breathed an audible sigh of relief as high fives were exchanged in the cockpit and the cabin, where the rest of the major's team were gathered near the door, listening to the proceedings.

Former Major Anokhin killed the mood. "Without the tanker, we need to land as quickly as possible."

Kozhin frowned, but nodded. "Unfortunately, you're right. We still have the contingency plan for this possibility, so I guess we'll have to use it."

"Agreed. The question is where."

Kozhin turned to the pilot. "Where do we have enough fuel to reach?"

The pilot double-checked the gauge. "Barely enough to make it back to Russia."

Kozhin waved his hand. "No way are we going there. As soon as we're over Russian airspace, they'll probably shoot us down."

Anokhin grunted. "They'll wait until we're on the ground."

Kozhin's eyes narrowed and he glanced over his shoulder at Anokhin. "Why?"

"They'll want to save the plane. It's expensive."

Kozhin chuckled. "You're probably right. Either way, we're dead." He turned back to the pilot. "Where else?"

"Iceland, Greenland?"

Anokhin dismissed the suggestions. "We may escape the plane, but we'll never get off the islands. We don't have any contacts there."

Kozhin hated that the man was right.

"Most of Europe."

Anokhin nodded. "Probably our best bet."

The pilot disagreed. "My money's on Canada or the United States. Preferably Canada."

Kozhin's eyebrows shot up. "United States? Are you kidding? We've been holding them over a barrel for hours."

"Which is why I said preferably Canada. The contingency requires you to get on the ground and disappear. Canada is sparsely populated, especially compared to the east coast of the United States. The moment your feet hit the ground in the US, there'll be a hundred guns pointed at each of your heads. If we execute our plan in Canada, you might just get away."

Kozhin's head slowly bobbed. The pilot was right. Europe was extremely densely populated—there was no escaping there. The United

States, at least where they could reach, was the same. But Canada? From his understanding, most of the east coast was barely populated, perhaps a couple of million people over hundreds of thousands of square miles.

His decision was made.

He turned to Anokhin. "Make the arrangements."

"Yes, sir."

One of his men appeared. "Sir, there's an incoming call."

Kozhin's eyebrows shot up. "Who? General Gorokhin is dead. It's not those idiots in the Azores, is it?"

"No, sir. It's coming over a Russian Air Force frequency, but he claims to be the President of the United States."

Kozhin cursed. "I guess the Kremlin is cooperating. Let's see what he has to say, and let him think *we're* cooperating." He followed Anokhin's man to the communications center and fit the headphones over his ears. "Mr. President, may I say it's an honor."

"Likewise, Mr. Kozhin."

Kozhin frowned, his identity no longer a secret, probably revealed before General Gorokhin's death. "So you know who I am."

"Indeed. And my people tell me you are running out of fuel."

Kozhin smiled. "You are well informed, Mr. President. But something tells me you didn't call just to chitchat."

"No, I didn't. I called to tell you that if you detonate any other cables, I have given my pilots permission to remove you from the sky."

Kozhin smiled. "I would expect no less, now that I have no options."

"I'm glad we understand each other."

"We do, Mr. President. I suppose there is no possibility of negotiating for leniency?"

"Land, hand yourself over to the authorities, and we'll discuss it."

Kozhin chuckled. "Mr. President, I do believe that's the first time you've lied to me."

Conference Room 212, CIA Headquarters

Langley, Virginia

"Mr. President, the plane is changing heading. It looks like they're now tracking toward the east coast."

Cheers and clapping erupted around the room, and Leroux suppressed a smile. While this was a minor victory, it wasn't as if some global disaster had been averted, or thousands of lives had been saved. Some technology had been saved. And money. But it wasn't as if the money would have been lost. It simply would have been spent on things that hadn't been planned for. The companies that laid the cables would be given juicy contracts to repair them, then more would be eventually laid to increase redundancies in the system. Profits would be made, taxes paid on those profits. New jobs would be created, income taxes paid on those salaries. The governments would get their money back.

Morrison cleared his throat, leaning forward at the boardroom table. "Mr. President, I think it's time we implement that contingency plan Mr. Leroux suggested."

President Starling nodded. "Do it."

The image from the Oval Office went dark, and the meeting broke, the orders issued for the contingency plan by the Joint Chief. Leroux left the room with Morrison, and they headed back toward Morrison's office.

"What does your gut tell you now?"

Leroux frowned. "The same as it did before. He's got a way out of this, and there's only one possibility I can think of."

"I hope you're wrong, otherwise our zero body count could go up."

Leroux pursed his lips. "There was a crew on that tanker."

"I don't include bad guys in my body counts."

Leroux chuckled. "Probably wise." They reached Morrison's outer office. "I'm going to return to the Ops Center and see if we can get a handle on who else was behind this."

Morrison paused. "What do you mean?"

Leroux shrugged. "Somebody had to plant the bombs."

East of the Azores, Atlantic Ocean

Thatcher sat in his cabin, pulling at his hair as he rocked back and forth. Everything was falling apart. Everything he had dreamed of was no more. Fleming had said he heard gunshots, which likely meant Spud and Tark were dead—they couldn't reach either of their cellphones, and had stopped trying once they realized that perhaps the authorities had them and they could be traced.

And if that were the case, it was likely too late for him and his remaining crew.

He had already posted a message on a private Internet group to the other teams, telling them what was going on, and to go into hiding. Their website and anything else that might incriminate them was being removed, but it would at best delay their capture. They had never hidden who they were—after all, until these past few days, they had never done anything illegal. They were advocates, at worst agitators.

Yet they had crossed a line when this new plan had become possible. And they had done it willingly. They all agreed to the plan unanimously, and were all prepared to be arrested. The publicity surrounding it would have furthered their cause.

But now nothing had been accomplished, and they were all going to jail uselessly. They'd be labeled terrorists, and nobody would pay them any mind.

A gentle knock on his hatch had him wiping the tears that had run unnoticed down his cheeks. "Yeah?"

The door opened and Giselle stepped inside. Her eyes were red, her dark cheeks stained. "Can I come in?"

He nodded. "Yeah, misery loves company."

She smiled weakly and closed the hatch, joining him on his cot. "What's going to happen?"

He sighed, leaning against the bulkhead. "We're going to be arrested and thrown in prison, and no one is going to have even heard our message."

She pushed back against the wall then leaned on him, resting her head on his shoulder. "This sucks."

He grunted. "Yeah, that's the understatement of the year."

She drew her legs up under her. "I'm going to miss you."

He put his arm around her and squeezed. "I'm going to miss you too. Something tells me that after today, we're never going to see each other again."

She looked up at him. "Surely that can't be true."

He shrugged. "Prisons aren't exactly coed. Maybe we'll see each other at the trial, but after that…" He sighed. "You know, I always liked you."

She squirmed closer. "I know."

He chuckled. "You did?"

"You're pretty easy to read."

He frowned. "Oh, well, sorry if I made you uncomfortable."

She patted his leg. "If you had, I would have told you. You know me."

"Yeah, I guess I do."

"Why didn't you ever make a move?"

He grunted. "I guess I was always intimidated by you."

"Now it's my turn to be sorry." She looked up at him, her eyes narrowing. "You know, come to think of it, I don't think I've *ever* seen you with a woman."

He smiled slightly at her, staring at her beautiful face. "I've only ever had eyes for you."

Hers widened. "You mean you've been single for over seven years because you've had a thing for me, and you never acted on it?"

He blushed, turning away. "Yeah, I guess I've been a fool." He felt her hand on his cheek, pulling his face back toward her.

"Yes, you have. All you had to do was ask."

He stared into her eyes. "You were way out of my league. Still are."

She smiled at him. "Always underestimating yourself. That's one of the things I like about you." She closed her eyes and leaned in, sending his heart pounding. He stared at her, unsure of what to do, then took the plunge.

He kissed her, and his heart raced faster as it grew more passionate, seven years of fantasies and built-up frustrations finally being realized and released. He didn't care if she loved him like he loved her, all he cared about was that in this moment, they were together, doing what he had always dreamed of doing from the moment she had introduced herself all those years ago.

She pushed him back on the bed and wrapped her leg around him as they lay on their sides, their bodies intertwining until he knew his ultimate fantasy was about to come true. She stared into his eyes, and he smiled.

"I love you."

She smiled, kissing him hard, but saying nothing. It was too much to ask that she love him back, and it hurt for a moment, maybe even a little longer. She was here to forget her own pain, her own disappointment, and do something nice for him. Perhaps in time, she would love him too, and he could wait.

Yet there was no time to wait.

All they would probably have was this moment. For before the day was out, their lives as they knew them would be over, and he would never see the love of his life again.

Approaching the Eastern Seaboard, United States

Niner felt ready to pass out as he pulled as hard as he could along with Jimmy and Spock. "Give, you bastard!"

Atlas seemed as cool as a cucumber on a Sunday stroll, if cucumbers could take strolls, not even a bead of sweat on his forehead. "Are you three ready to give up yet?"

"Never surrender! Never say die!" cried Niner as he leaned back, putting all his body weight and muscle power into the effort. Spock and Jimmy joined him, all three of them now hanging onto Atlas' hand and forearm, putting all of their nearly six hundred pounds of body weight into it, and still the big man's arm didn't budge. Dawson stepped into the room and shook his head at the sight.

"I think BD has something to say," said Atlas, who ended the three-on-one arm wrestling match with one swift motion that had his opponents tumbling toward him. "Oh, and I think all three of you losers owe me twenty bucks each."

Niner stood, gasping for breath, his hands on his knees, as he cocked his head to the side, staring at Atlas. "I want him cut open so we can make sure he's not some sort of Terminator under all that bulk."

Atlas kissed his bicep. "Nothin' but American made and Army trained muscle under here." He gave Niner the stink eye. "What's your excuse?"

Niner, still bent over, freed one hand to flip him the bird. Dawson closed the door.

"Hate to break up the fun—though with the humiliating display I just saw, perhaps I should have shown up earlier—but we've been called up again. Our friends at the CIA have a crazy theory, and we're being diverted just in case they're right."

Sergeant Will "Spock" Lightman cocked an eyebrow. "What's the theory?"

"You're going to like it." Dawson turned to Red. "We'll be dropping you and five guys in Halifax, where you're going to rendezvous with a Canadian JTF2 team, just in case the CIA is wrong and they attempt a landing in Canada. We think they're almost out of fuel, so won't have a lot of choices. You'll deploy from there as necessary."

Red smiled. "Always fun to work with some Crazy Canucks."

Niner raised a hand. "Can I go with Red? I still want to know what the hell a BeaverTail is."

Dawson nodded. "Fine. Don't come back until you find out."

"Or just don't come back," rumbled Atlas.

Niner pouted at him. "You're so mean to me that I know you care." He leaped over the table and hugged him. "Forget BeaverTails! I'm sticking with you!"

Off the coast of Pico Island, Azores

Thatcher sucked in a quick breath as he awoke, the changing sound of the engines likely the cause. He smiled at the naked form of Giselle, curled up at his side, her head on his shoulder, a smile on her face.

He loved her.

He had almost from the moment he had met her. And it was never meant to be, but at least he'd spend the rest of his life behind bars with the memories of their lovemaking, an experience that was every bit as good as he imagined.

They just meshed.

And it made it all the more heartbreaking that it was never to happen again. He lay his head back on the pillow, listening to the sounds of activity outside, when a thought occurred to him.

Nobody was dead.

Yes, he was quite certain that some of their team were dead in Portugal, but no innocents were dead. All they had done was plant some explosives on data cables. Kozhin had detonated them, not his people. And even if found equally to blame, how many years in prison could that be? When murderers didn't get imprisoned for life, how many years could they truly be sentenced? Five? Ten? He looked at Giselle and smiled.

Maybe there's a chance for us yet.

He sighed. The engines were idling now, indicating they had obviously reached their destination. He wasn't sure why he had ordered their return to the Azores site, as there was nothing they could actually do, but he wasn't thinking rationally. At least he wasn't a couple of hours ago when he had given the order. And now that he was, an unfortunate thought occurred to him.

There *was* something he could do.

He brushed some hairs from Giselle's forehead and she moaned, snuggling closer though remaining asleep. There was one last, foolish thing he could do, but it would mean saying goodbye to Giselle forever.

And that was something he could never imagine himself doing.

Giselle rolled over and stretched, groaning in ecstasy, though not as intensely as earlier. It had been wonderful, and just what she had needed. She didn't love Thatcher, but she did care for him, and liked him tremendously. In time, she could definitely see herself falling for him, though because he had never made a move on her, the nature of their relationship had become one of platonic friends, at least from her side of things.

She knew he liked her, though a lot of men did—she was unique— or at least different from most women these guys were used to. Her dark skin and big hair with Grace Jones makeup balanced with Tomboyish clothes, made her an eclectic mix of the exotic and forbidden.

But she never got the impression Thatcher just wanted to "try her out." And their lovemaking session of earlier was proof of that. It was gentle and slow, not some frantic session of porn positions. He had stared into her eyes the entire time, had made her feel loved, and had shown that he hoped this would be something they'd do together every day for the rest of their lives.

She sighed. If being with him meant feeling the way she had earlier, then she could imagine a lot worse, and little better. She sat up, finally realizing she was alone in the narrow bed. She looked about the cabin, then spotted a folded note sitting atop her clothes on a nearby chair. She smiled when she spotted her name on the front.

She rose, the sheet gripped against her naked body, and grabbed the note, sitting back down and unfolding it. Her smile turned to a frown as she read what was written, then she burst from the edge of the bed, rushing out of the cabin and onto the deck. "Where's Thatch?"

The others in sight stared at her naked body, mouths agape for a moment.

"Where is he?" she demanded, suddenly aware she was naked, but not caring in the slightest.

Fleming pointed at the water. "He went over about five minutes ago."

Her eyes widened. "To do what?"

Fleming shrugged. "Dunno. I figured he'd have told you."

He hadn't, but the sickening pit in her stomach told her exactly what he planned.

As did the last lines in his letter to her.

I'm so happy my last memories will be of staring into your eyes. I love you, Thatch.

Operations Center 3, CIA Headquarters

Langley, Virginia

"Hey, boss, got something."

Leroux glanced over at Child. "What is it?"

"Something just got posted onto social media, referencing the cables." He tapped a few keys then nodded toward the displays at the front of the operations center. A video appeared, one man sitting in a chair, staring at the camera, the room behind him empty.

"My name is Gavin Thatcher. I'm the founder of Step Back Now. Many of you have no doubt heard the reports of transatlantic data cables being destroyed as part of an extortion attempt by Konstantin Kozhin. I want everyone to know that Step Back Now did indeed plant the bombs, but extortion was not our motive. Kozhin betrayed us. Our goal was to sever all the cables at once, and stimulate conversation on either side of the Atlantic. Our intent was to send the message that follows this one that I am recording now, to make people think about the harm they are doing to themselves, and society, by burying their heads behind their phones, and living their lives on the Internet, rather than in the real world.

"But our message has been lost to the greed of Mr. Kozhin, who stole our pure intent, and twisted it into the age-old sin of greed. It's for this reason that I take this action today. Our message needs to get out, and there is only one way to stimulate that conversation. I can no longer sever all the cables that join our two continents, as the control lies with Mr. Kozhin. But I can sever one of them, and in so doing, I hope my sacrifice will draw the attention of the world, and stimulate that conversation I had hoped would occur had our original plans unfolded the way they were meant to. I do this not for me, but for you. There is still time to save yourselves, to save humanity. Come out from behind the screens, and embrace your fellow man."

Tears filled the man's eyes, and Leroux stepped closer, his expert mind reading every facial cue and body movement as the manifesto continued.

"Say hello to the person you catch a glimpse of every day in the line at the coffee shop, rather than stare at the cold piece of technology gripped in your hand." His voice cracked. "Feel the touch of someone you love, rather than its unfeeling stiffness. Live the life you were meant to live, not the life corporations designed for you." He closed his eyes for a moment, then opened them. "I do this for the one I love."

The screen went black and the room remained silent as everyone waited for someone else to say something. Leroux had to admit he was moved by the emotion displayed, but that wasn't his job. His job was to stop what the man was about to do. He turned to face his team.

"I think it's clear from that message that he intends to detonate the Azores device. Just in case we're the first to see this, notify the Portuguese authorities and tell them what's going on, and I'll notify the Director that Mr. Kozhin is not responsible for the explosion that's about to happen, so he can advise the President to not blow him out of the sky for violating the agreement."

Child raised his hand. "Umm, boss?"

Leroux turned to him. "Yes?"

"There might be a problem."

"What's that?"

"The professors just landed in the Azores, and if we know them…"

Leroux cursed. "They're going to try and stop him."

EQ Hotel & Casino
Shanghai, China

"We have it."

Kane smiled in the mirror, his earpiece, shoved so far into his ear canal it was invisible to the naked eye, relaying the critical update from his team. He spit the toothpaste into the sink, not responding, a camera hidden behind the mirror in front of him. He swished some mouthwash then gargled, again spitting, then wiped his mouth dry, giving the mirror a grin to check his teeth. "The good news is, I'm a handsome devil." He held up his deodorant stick. "On to stage two!" He began applying it, then his cologne.

"Stage two has been initiated. Mr. Zhang's yacht has just been reported found in Macao."

Kane gave two thumbs up to the mirror, knowing his team, and Zhang's men, were monitoring the feed. He stepped out of the steamed up bathroom, and smiled at Tien humming happily in the next room.

Last night had been a lot of fun, a great deal of pleasure taken in knowing he had saved the poor girl from at least one night of having to service one of Zhang's clients or henchmen.

He put his watch on and entered a sequence to activate it, and was rewarded with a series of pulses indicating a message. He grabbed his phone and stepped out on the balcony with a cigarette. He checked the message from Leroux and cursed. Acton was apparently storming into danger again, probably unarmed, and there was nothing he could do about it. If anything, the CIA's warning to him probably only egged the man on further.

He shook his head, then stared out at the city below, thinking how easy it should be for Tien to lose herself among the millions. But without resources, without contacts, there was nothing she could do.

And it ate him up.

"Tien!"

The diminutive woman appeared in his bedroom door and he waved at her through the glass. She smiled and stepped onto the balcony. He beckoned her to join him in the corner, out of sight of the camera. "Speak very low, otherwise they can hear us."

Her eyes bulged, a hint of fear on her face, but she nodded.

"Where are you from originally?"

"Vietnam."

"How did you get here?"

Her eyes widened even further. "I-I was kidnapped when I crossed the border to sell our fruit in the market."

"So your family is still there?"

254

She shrugged. "I hope so."

"If you were given the chance, would you go back?"

Her head drooped. "I can never go back. They told me they'd kill me and my family if I ever tried."

Kane tensed, a rage forming in his stomach. "I understand." He put an arm around her. "Did I hear you say breakfast arrived?"

She forced a smile. "Yes."

"Great, I'm starved. Let's eat!"

Pico Airport

Pico Island, Azores

Acton rushed down the steps of the Gulf V, the SUV they had rented earlier waiting for them, somebody from the hotel holding the keys with a smile. Laura's travel agent Mary was incredible, never failing to impress.

"Thanks!" He grabbed the keys, climbing in the driver's seat, Reading shotgun, with Laura and Spencer occupying the back. He fired up the engine and chirped the tires as he accelerated away from the terminal and toward their dive site. Reading leaned forward and placed a hand on his shoulder.

"Slow down, you're liable to get us killed, or worse, some innocent bystander. Besides, what do you plan on doing when you get there?"

Acton eased off the gas slightly, then a lot when he came around a blind corner and nearly rear-ended a sedan. Reading was right. What could he do? He couldn't defuse a bomb, he couldn't risk his life diving over two hundred feet below the surface to fight an unknown number of people under the water, especially people who had a submersible with robot arms. "I can direct the authorities, if necessary."

Reading leaned back. "Yes, that *is* something you can do. But the update from the CIA said they had notified the authorities of the location of the suspects' boat, and that we were advised to back off."

His friend was only trying to help, but Acton was getting frustrated regardless. If that bomb went off, there was no saying what it could do to the discovery. He wasn't even sure it was Atlantis, but if the trident had been discovered by accident, surely there were other artifacts buried under the accumulation of silt that could provide further evidence of either what city Niner had discovered, or whether Atlantis did actually exist, somewhere. He couldn't let anything happen to it.

They reached the coastal road and Laura pointed to the ocean. "Look!"

Several boats with lights flashing were racing along with them, the Portuguese evidently not only having received the update from the CIA, but deciding to act on it. It gave Acton hope, and an irrational part of him wished they boarded the hostile's boat with the same ferocity as their own liberators back on the mainland.

A wave of regret swept over him as he pictured the simple, friendly man the others had called Spud, and the innocent brother, dragged into a conspiracy merely because he was born into the same family as a zealot.

"I can't believe someone is doing all this because they have a hate-on for Facebook."

Acton glanced at Spencer in the rearview mirror, but said nothing. The boy was right. It was ridiculous, if that were all it was. On the plane, they had heard the final words of a desperate man, then the message that had originally been meant to be sent, the video already trending worldwide and leading every newscast.

He actually agreed with their message.

He avoided Facebook as much as he could, had deleted his LinkedIn and Twitter accounts years ago, and had never even created an account for Snapchat, Pinterest, Instagram, and whatever else the kids were using these days to hide their activity from their parents.

He preferred human contact.

Face-to-face.

He had taken to text messaging, as it was convenient in many instances, but he still preferred to pick up the phone and call someone. He always found it at once amusing and dismaying at how awkward so many millennials sounded on the phone, their inexperience with the medium tragic. These terrorists—he hesitated to use the word since they weren't out killing in the name of their god—had a message that deserved to be heard, but their methods could never be condoned.

And the unintended consequences of what he feared their leader, Thatcher, was about to do, could be tragic.

He had to be stopped.

The question was who was going to do it.

Off the coast of Pico Island, Azores

Giselle had been shoved back in her cabin by Fleming, but not before running around the entire deck of their boat, screaming for someone to do something.

"Put some clothes on, for God's sake!"

She had wanted to react with rage, but instead realized Fleming was right, the men not answering her, instead drinking in her body. Nudity had never been much of a thing for her, her parents free spirits, the naked form nothing to be shocked over. At the appropriate time, it should be enjoyed and partaken of, but this was not that time.

She emerged from the cabin, dressed, and headed for the rear deck. "Has anyone reached him?"

Fleming looked at her. "Yes, he's responding, but he's not turning back."

Giselle pointed at the submersible. "Get it in the water."

"Why?"

"Because somebody has to stop him."

Approaching Newfoundland & Labrador, Canada

"Sir, we're approaching the coast."

Kozhin nodded at Anokhin and rose, following him to the rear of the aircraft. The mercenaries, with the exception of the pilot and copilot, were gathered, all now dressed in civilian attire, no longer in their private contractor gear.

Anokhin presented two of his men. "They will be diving with you. They are two of my best. We've already confirmed the boat is in position to meet you. They'll guide you down. Just remain calm, remember what I've told you, listen to them, and you'll come out of this no problem."

Kozhin looked at him. "I still think we should all be going."

Anokhin shook his head. "No, a large group will draw too much attention. And don't forget, we have our own contingency."

Kozhin nodded, trying to keep a brave face on for the sake of the alpha males that surrounded him. He had never been one to consider himself a coward, then again, he had never done what he was about to do. It was insane, and once again he questioned whether he should go forward with it. So he'd spend some time in prison. Big deal. He could do the time, especially with the money he had.

They'll probably deport you to Russia.

He frowned at the memory of Anokhin's words. Russian prison was *not* something he could survive. The horror stories of the modern gulags were bone-chilling, and even those with money who had challenged the almighty leader, were rotting, their billions unable to even ease their suffering. He drew a deep breath and squared his shoulders.

"Let's get this over with."

Dawson checked his gear once again, readying for what the CIA had suggested might be the endgame move of their target, one Konstantin Kozhin. The man had quite the file, his father an even thicker one, and had a history of going to the extremes when in tight quarters—and none were tighter than he was in now.

He had been found out, betrayed by General Gorokhin in his final moments, resulting in him being trapped in a tin can in the sky. While it was an interesting idea to run the operation from a Russian Air Force plane over the middle of the Atlantic Ocean, it left few options if one were discovered.

Which meant he had a contingency plan.

The Russians had confirmed the plane wasn't manned by their people, which likely meant mercenaries. The CIA had found out that Kozhin had dealings with Medved Corps, a group made up mostly of ex-soldiers, many of whom were Spetsnaz—Russian Special Forces. They were good at their jobs, and would have planned for such a scenario, even if Kozhin hadn't.

His comm crackled in his ear. "They're descending. Stand by."

Dawson stood and stretched, turning to the others. "Looks like our friends at the Agency might be right. Check your gear, and be ready for a fight."

The others all rose and Dawson inspected Spock's gear then he did the same for him. A slap on the back had him turning to face his men. "If this goes down the way I think it will, we eliminate the escort first, then Kozhin only if necessary.

Spock cocked an eyebrow. "And how are we supposed to know who's who?"

Dawson smiled slightly. "My guess is he'll be either the one without a gun, or the one who doesn't know how to use it. Nothing in his file indicates he has any experience."

Atlas grunted. "Files have been known to be wrong."

Dawson shrugged. "Then we shoot them all, and sort it out later."

Kozhin stood while Anokhin checked his gear one last time. "Are you ready?"

Kozhin frowned. "Hell, no. But let's do this anyway."

Anokhin grinned at him. "That's the spirit!" Anokhin nodded at one of his men, and a door was opened to the outside. The cabin temperature rapidly dropped as the wind whistled around them. Kozhin turned to face the door and his two escorts each took one of his arms, leading him to the doorframe, the rugged landscape of a chilly Newfoundland below them. He closed his eyes and began to feel dizzy.

Not a wise choice.

He opened them and his equilibrium returned. A light turned green to his left and the first man stepped out, pulling him with him, Kozhin's pilot chute in the second man's hand.

"Arch!"

He completely forgot his brief verbal training, unsure of what to do, when he heard the single word yelled again. He thrust his arms and legs out and shoved his head and shoulders back, arching his spine.

Suddenly he heard a flutter above him then a jerk as the pilot chute dragged his main open, killing his speed. He took a moment to orient himself, grabbing his straps velcroed above him, and confirmed a good chute.

That was the end of what he was responsible for.

The plane roared away rapidly and two fighter jets broke off their pursuit, slowly circling this new development, no doubt radioing in the fact three people were now under parachutes, about to set foot on Canadian territory.

A rumble above and to his right had his head swiveling to figure out the source.

And he cursed.

Dawson dove out the aft baggage door of the Gulfstream G550 first, the others following rapidly. As he dove, his arms at his sides to increase his speed and close the gap with the enemy, he gave silent kudos to whoever at the CIA had figured out what the contingency plan might be.

What was surprising was that only three had made their escape. There had to be more on the plane. Kozhin would have no clue how to operate it, and there was no way two men could operate everything.

The three chutes below him were rapidly approaching. He could overshoot them and just meet them on the ground, but that would give the hostiles too many opportunities to shoot out their canopies from above.

"Deploy now." He pulled his chute, the others around him doing the same, then prepared his MP5 as he double-checked his canopy overhead. "Control, Zero-One. Be advised, only three hostiles left the plane. Over."

"Copy that, Zero-One. Will advise Zero-Two's team. Out."

Dawson took aim at the first chute on the left, trying to figure out which one was Kozhin.

"Look out!" cried Kozhin as he spotted six chutes deploying above them. Both his escorts looked up and weapons were pulled. Gunfire erupted from both, and Kozhin watched with satisfaction as a chute overhead was shredded, the man dangling under the canopy now rapidly descending.

Gunfire from overhead responded, and Kozhin turned his attention to the ground as they closed in on it. He could see a boat matching the description he had been given, near the shoreline. They were supposed to land then make their way to the shore where they'd be taken to the larger vessel. They would then steam into international waters, and onto a cargo vessel that would take them to Europe and its masses crammed into beautiful, open borders.

But all of that could only happen if they could get to the ground alive, and onto the boat. Something loud erupted below them, bright flashes coming from the deck of the boat bringing a smile to his face.

Dawson cursed as he dropped, his MP5 belching lead at the two armed men below him, the others joining in. The hostiles' chutes were quickly shredded, but that wasn't enough. As they lost their lift, they dropped toward the ground like he was, and he kept pace, leaving what was left of his chute still deployed rather than cutting it loose. He wanted to control his descent at least somewhat, because once he deployed his reserve, that was it.

No third chances.

One of the hostiles shook several times as Dawson's aim was true, then the other, someone on his team taking the final gun out of the equation. He was about to cut loose his torn chute when he heard the distinctive sound of a .50 caliber from far below.

"It's coming from that boat!"

Dawson searched for the boat Spock was referring to and spotted it, muzzle flashes erupting from its deck. "Break away, I'll take care of it."

Dawson pulled the release, his useless chute tearing away, and he dropped. Leaning forward, he gained speed, his arms crossed over his chest as he held his weapon tight against his body so it didn't tear free and knock him out.

He blasted past the only remaining hostile's chute, the man unarmed, or at least not partaking in the battle that had just taken place, so most likely Kozhin. He could see three men on the deck now, one operating the .50, another feeding it ammo, the third with a pair of binoculars finding the targets.

And apparently ignoring the free-falling body they assumed was dead.

That should do it.

Dawson pulled his reserve, the speed and size of the chute resulting in a bone-wrenching jolt, something he had felt hundreds of times before in training and on missions. He gripped his MP5 tight, raising it to take aim, when the man with the binoculars suddenly spotted him. He could hear the shouts above the surf below, and the barrel of the machine gun turned toward him.

Dawson squeezed the trigger, pouring lead on the deck. The man feeding the ammo was hit first, and Dawson adjusted left, the next few bursts eliminating the threat, the final ones sending the spotter over the side. The engine fired up and Dawson banked to his right, taking aim at the bridge, opening fire and shattering the windows. A body slumped forward and into sight as he rapidly closed the distance between himself and the boat.

He kept his weapon aimed, his eyes searching for any movement, then mere feet from the deck, reached up and flared his chute, trimming his speed. He hit the deck hard and rolled with a grunt, immediately regaining a knee, scanning left to right for any movement. Finding none, he freed himself of his chute, letting it flutter away, eventually landing in the roiling ocean.

He cleared the deck, making sure the two manning the weapon were indeed dead, then killed the engine before performing a quick search of the vessel, finding no one else on board. Back on the deck, he stared up at the sky to see one lone chute about to land nearby on the shore, and five more chutes closing in. He smiled as he fired up the engine, making for land.

Try to take him alive, boys.

Kozhin closed his eyes, pulling down on his toggles as he had been told to do. He felt himself float back up and the sensation sent butterflies through his stomach.

Then he slammed hard into the rocky ground, the sensation merely an illusion.

Keep your eyes open at all times.

Anokhin's warning echoed too late through his head, and as he struggled to his feet, trying to reel the chute in, he wondered what he was supposed to do next. He stared down at his chest and pulled at the buckle. The harness released and he shrugged out of the chute.

Something fluttered overhead and he looked up, cursing as he spotted the team sent to capture him coming in for a landing. An engine roared to his right and he turned, smiling as he spotted the boat he was to rendezvous with, racing for the shore. He sprinted over the craggy landscape, toward salvation. If he could get to the boat first, he just might escape these insane men who had jumped out of an airplane to pursue him.

"Halt!"

He glanced over his shoulder to see the first of his enemy touch down. Kozhin's foot stubbed a rock and he stumbled, falling headlong onto the unforgiving ground. He cursed, his body screaming out in pain, but he pushed to his feet.

He wasn't going to prison.

Not today.

He willed himself forward, the boat now at the shoreline. He would be there in less than a minute. He just had to keep going. He waved at the pilot as he emerged from the bridge, then nearly cried out in disappointment, the man in what appeared to be a US Military uniform with a weapon strapped to his chest, returning the wave with a big smile.

Kozhin slowed then stopped, his shoulders slumping as his knees gave out. He collapsed to the ground, the sounds of heavy footfalls behind him easing, the chase over. He stared up at the heavens, his heart heavy.

Please don't let them put me in a Russian prison.

Director Morrison's Office, CIA Headquarters
Langley, Virginia

National Clandestine Service Chief Leif Morrison grabbed his phone, the call his aide had announced, unexpected. "Petra! What can I do for you?"

"There's something I think you need to know that might assist you in the apprehension of Mr. Kozhin and his people."

Morrison bit his tongue, deciding he wanted to hear what she was about to say, rather than inform her that Kozhin had been captured only moments ago, and that the Il-80 was just about to land in Goose Bay, Labrador.

"What's that?"

"In the past several weeks, General Gorokhin arranged for a number of diplomatic passports."

Morrison's mouth opened slightly as he leaned back in his chair. "So *that's* how they plan on getting away with it. Diplomatic immunity."

"Exactly."

"And is your government going to honor these documents?"

"You know the Kremlin never tolerates the abuse of its citizens beyond its borders."

Morrison frowned. "You didn't answer my question, Petra."

She sighed. "Even I'm surprised by the answer, my friend."

CFB Goose Bay

Newfoundland & Labrador, Canada

Anokhin checked his tie. Everyone was in civilian business attire, all of their private weapons and equipment tossed over the Gulf of St. Lawrence between the island of Newfoundland and the mainland of Labrador, any weapons remaining Russian Army issue. There would be nothing incriminating found on board, and with their diplomatic passports in hand, legally, the aircraft couldn't even be searched.

The pilot brought the massive craft to a halt and powered down the engines on Canadian soil, the decision having been made quite early on that there was no way they would land in the United States. At least with Canada, their diplomatic rights would be honored, and they'd probably be on a plane to Moscow within days, if not hours.

But in the United States? They might be shot the moment their feet hit the tarmac.

Anokhin opened the door, muttering a curse as a Siberia-worthy wind howled into the cabin. He turned to the others. "It's like Mother Russia out there, boys!"

Laughter greeted him, and he was pleased to see his men were in good spirits. They were about to get away with some pretty serious crimes. He had no doubt when they were returned to Russia, there would be some questions asked, but they were contractors for Medved Corps, linked very tightly with the Kremlin, and too many generals and admirals to count. Publicly they might be condemned, but they wouldn't serve a day behind bars, and would be back at work on Monday.

Russia loved its heroes, and anyone who stuck it to the West was a hero, especially these days with the elected dictator controlling the message its citizens were allowed to hear. Russia was strong again, and that was a good thing, but even he had to admit at times that it was Stalin strong, not Communist Party strong. The Soviet Union after Stalin had been essentially led by committee. Today's Russia was again led by someone who wouldn't hesitate to kill his enemies in gruesomely public ways, assert his will over helpless states, and publicly ridicule anyone who dared challenge him.

Russia was powerful, but at what cost?

Which was why he kept his money in Swiss accounts, not Russian. One day, the other shoe would drop, and he had no intention of being around to be squashed by it.

He tapped his handgun stuffed into his belt, and stepped into the winter that awaited them outside, half a dozen heavily armed soldiers, their weapons aimed at them, spread out to greet them.

He held up his red diplomatic passport. "Pavel Anokhin. I have diplomatic immunity, as do my companions."

One of the soldiers stepped forward, his shaved head covered by an ever-increasing helping of snow. "I have been instructed to inform you that Moscow has revoked all diplomatic passports issued by General Gorokhin, including yours and those of your men. Cooperate, and you'll survive the day, sir. Now, all of you, on your knees, hands on your head!"

Anokhin stared at the man, still processing what he had just heard. Could he be telling the truth? Could Moscow have revoked the passports? The fact these men knew that General Gorokhin was involved, proved that he had indeed been compromised. But would Russia abandon its citizens so easily?

He couldn't see it. Something was going on here, and he wasn't about to let these soldiers, who appeared to be a mix of Canadian and American, dictate the terms.

He slowly raised his hands, backing away from their hosts, and toward the aircraft. "Get back on board," he whispered in Russian.

The bald man responded, in perfect Russian. "That's not going to help you, sir."

Anokhin continued his slow retreat, a smile spreading. "You speak Russian."

"Know thine enemy."

"Are we your enemy? I thought we were friends."

The bald man shrugged. "We tried it for a while. You guys decided you didn't like it." He raised his weapon slightly. "Now stop moving, or I help you stop moving."

"You'd shoot an unarmed man?"

The man tapped his ear. "All of your men have been identified. Your file has been read to me while we've been standing here. Even in your skivvies, you're armed."

Anokhin grabbed his package. "You have *this* in your file."

The man chuckled. "I think you know what I mean."

Anokhin reached the steps of the plane, his men flanking him on either side. "I think our conversation is over."

"Take one step onto that plane, and I put you down."

Anokhin sneered at him. "I don't think you have the balls." He put his foot on the first step and a shot rang out, a hole torn into the fuselage, just to the right of his head.

I guess we do this the hard way.

He reached behind his back and pulled his gun, the others doing the same.

Niner lay prone on the roof of Hangar 7, overlooking the tarmac and the proceedings below, Jimmy at his side. "Well, that's disappointing." He squeezed the trigger, the target on the far right dropping, the red mist of what were once organs and other vital tissues now decorating the fuselage of the Il-80. Another shot from his left rang out from the Canadian sniper team, the target on the far left down.

Niner already had the second target on the right lined up, and he squeezed the trigger as the guest of honor's weapon appeared and his body shook repeatedly as the half-dozen men on the tarmac opened fire.

It was over in seconds, and not a single hostile had got off a shot.

Niner rolled onto his back, staring up at the snow gently floating down from above. He activated his comm. "Charlie Zero-One, this is Bravo One-One. I think it's time for BeaverTails, over."

His comm squelched. "One-One, the only beaver tails you're getting here are the real thing. Next time I'm in Bragg, I'll bring you some. Out."

Niner frowned. "I think he's lying about the BeaverTails. I think they have them here."

Jimmy sat beside him, cross-legged. "I think you have to let it go."

Niner looked up at his friend. "Never surrender! Never say die!"

Pico Island, Azores

Thatcher continued his descent, the GPS on his suit indicating he was almost at the device. It had been a heart-wrenching decision to leave Giselle, to choose what he was about to do over a possible lifetime with her.

But choosing her would be selfish—he was put on this earth for a greater cause.

He had to save it from itself.

The action he was about to take would be even more effective than if the original plan had been executed as intended, if they hadn't been betrayed by that bastard Kozhin. This one act of defiance against the social media machine would send shockwaves around the world as people realized he had done it for them, and if even just one person put down their phone, and talked to the person beside them on the bus, or in the line to get their coffee, talked to them about what he had done for them, he would have succeeded in some small way to change their lives.

If just two people rediscovered the joy of having a face-to-face conversation, of reading genuine facial cues rather than emoticons, of luxuriating in the rhythm and pattern of speech, the inflections and tics, the extraneous words and sounds inserted to fill gaps while they searched for the next word.

The beautiful experience of conversation.

For millennia, man had struggled to find methods to communicate more effectively with each other, and just when they had finally perfected it through vocalized speech, they were destroying it with technology that eliminated all the humanity.

He spotted the cable ahead of him and his chest ached with the knowledge of what was about to happen, and the finality of his actions.

Suddenly a brilliant light shone at him from behind. He pushed with his arm and spun around, gasping at the sight of a submersible rushing toward him. Had the authorities found them? It was possible, and if they had, then he had failed even in this.

No!

He turned, kicking hard toward the cable and the explosive charge they had placed on it, when a voice came through his headgear. "Thatch, it's me, Giselle. What are you doing?"

He closed his eyes, the burn intense at the sound of her voice, the voice of an angel.

"Thatch! Please!"

He sighed, opening his eyes to find the submersible passing him then turning to block his path. He stopped, staring into the camera, a camera he knew was transmitting to the woman he loved. "Let me past, Giselle."

"I can't let you do it. It's not worth it!"

Her voice was cracking, and it made this all the more difficult. She cared. She didn't love him, but she cared.

Oh God, if she had only said she loved me!

It wouldn't have been true, but it would have been wonderful to hear, just once in his life.

Everyone deserves to be loved.

In all his years, no woman had ever said those three, beautiful, wonderful words. They had been sent insincerely through text messages from platonic friends, because electronically they were meaningless. But to have heard them in person, while staring into their eyes, hearing the breathless delivery—that would have been something to take to the grave.

He swam closer to the camera. "Let me do this, Giselle, let me make a difference. I can't take years in prison without you. Every day would be torture, and I don't want to go through that—it wouldn't be living, it would be merely existing. These past seven years with you have been incredible, and those moments we spent together earlier, were the most wonderful of my life. Thanks to you, I'll die a happy man, because I will have been with the woman I've loved for as long as I can remember, and I'll have sent a message to the world that will resonate throughout, and hopefully accomplish our goals." He reached for the camera, as if reaching for her hand. "I love you. Never forget that. Now please, let me finish what I started, what we all started."

He could hear her sobs through the headgear, and it broke his heart. Then there was a final sniff, and the whispered words that shattered his being, as he wasn't there to hear them in person.

"I love you too."

"Hang on!" Acton sent them careening around an unexpected corner before swiftly recovering, waving at two cars as they whipped by, horns and wagged middle fingers the response.

"Slow down or I'm going to have your license revoked."

Acton glanced over at Reading, wondering if the man was serious, when an exclamation of delight from the back seat ended the thought. "Did you connect?"

Laura nodded, her eyes glued to an iPad she had their travel agent Mary arrange with the hotel. "I've got the camera feeds coming through now."

"How's it look?"

"Everything appears the way we left it. If they've detonated, then it looks like the ruins have survived."

Acton wasn't so sure he was ready to declare victory just yet. "I don't think we're that lucky. My guess is they haven't had a chance yet. That means there's still hope."

Giselle's shoulders shook as she stared at the display, the man she only now realized she loved, pleading with her to let him kill himself. She hadn't been sure how she felt until she had been faced with the prospect of losing him, and the gut-wrenching feeling, a feeling that had almost made her vomit from the horror of it, convinced her that their friendship was no longer just that, that she shared his feelings, and she didn't want to live without him.

"I-I'm so happy to hear you say that. I wish I was there with you, so I could hold you, and say goodbye in person."

She stared at his beautiful face. "You still can. Just come back so we can be together one last time. Then if you decide you still want to do this, I-I'll come with you. We'll do it together."

She felt a hand grip her shoulder and she looked up at Fleming, tears streaking his face, and those surrounding her. She wished she were alone, but this was their moment too. The man who had brought them all together was about to sacrifice himself for the cause, for *their* cause, and they deserved to share in these final words, no matter how private, no matter how intimate.

And she loved each and every one of them for not saying anything to interrupt.

"Someone's coming!"

She heard the others head to the windows, but she ignored it. Her entire focus was on the man she loved.

"It's the police!"

"Break out the weapons!"

Footfalls pounded out of the room, and she found herself alone, finally.

"What's going on?"

She closed her eyes at the sounds of the sirens, and then the shouts over a megaphone, the words lost on her. "The police are here."

"Then you have to let me past, so I can finish this before they try and stop me."

"But I don't want you to die."

Gunfire erupted outside, sporadic at first, then more intense.

"Is that gunfire? Are you safe?"

"Don't worry about me. Just come up here, and we can be together."

An engine roared outside, then she felt a vibration through the deck plates as something hit the side of the vessel, the exchange of gunfire continuing.

"I think they're boarding us." She could see the anguish in his face.

"Tell them to surrender! No one was supposed to get hurt!"

Tears flowed down her cheeks. "You weren't supposed to get hurt, either."

He shook his head. "I'm making a choice. Now I need you to. Tell them to surrender, please!"

She closed her eyes as someone hammered at the hatch. "Goodbye, my love." She opened her eyes and saw a gun sitting beside the console. The door burst open, several police entering, and she made a decision. "I'll see you soon."

She reached for the gun.

"Giselle!"

Thatcher could hear the gunfire through his headgear, then a cry and a gasp. Footfalls echoed, then words he couldn't understand were said.

"Please! Can anyone hear me? Is Giselle okay?"

There was a pause, then a voice he didn't recognize replied. "This is the police. Where are you?"

Thatcher's chest tightened and his stomach drew into a tight knot. "Is she okay?"

"The girl is dead. I repeat, where are you?"

Thatcher's eyes closed as all will drained out of him. She was dead, and it was his fault. If he had never met Kozhin, if he had never agreed to move forward with this insane plan, if he had never met Giselle and invited her to join their group, she'd be alive today, somewhere out there in the world, happy, blissfully unaware that he even existed.

But that wasn't reality, and the reality he now faced was a world without the woman he loved in it. He opened his eyes, glaring at the submersible in front of him.

"Where you can't touch me."

He kicked to the right of the massive vehicle, pushing past it before someone up there figured out how to operate it. He kicked hard, the tears pouring down his cheeks making it difficult to see, wiping them clear impossible with his headgear on.

"Stop what you are doing!"

He ignored the voice, instead focusing on Giselle's precious gift to him.

I love you too.

He was going to die, but he was going to die having loved, and more importantly, having someone who loved him back. He hadn't believed her words at first, though he knew from those that followed that she truly did mean what she had said, and while those words were usually worth living for, they were the exact words he had needed to hear to give him the strength to die.

He reached the device and flipped open the panel protecting the detonator from stray debris accidentally activating it. He paused. "Are you listening?"

"Yes."

"Tell the world I did it for them."

He reached forward and pressed the button, ending a life well lived.

Acton cursed as he spotted a massive eruption of water to his left, his heart sinking at the realization the terrorists had made good on their threat. A horn blast and a shout from Reading had him swerve back onto his side of the road, the art of driving momentarily forgotten. He spotted an access point and cranked the wheel, sending everyone toward the passenger side as he surged onto the beach, racing toward the shore. He slammed on the brakes, skidding to a halt, then jumped out, rushing toward the water. He turned back, pointing at Laura.

"The cameras!"

She rushed over with the iPad and he stared at what appeared to be a steady image, the ruins untouched. He breathed a sigh of relief. "They're intact!" He grabbed Laura by the shoulders, squeezing her against him. "Oh, thank God!"

Then something moved.

It was a column, slowly tipping over, the water delaying the inexorable fall to the seabed, the massive piece of stone pounding into the surface with a puff of silt that spread out from all sides. Then another began to tip, and Acton's entire body tensed as a sickening feeling threatened to take over.

"Oh no!" gasped Laura, pointing at the screen. "What's happening?"

Acton wasn't sure. The image seemed to be shaking, as if the camera were vibrating, and everything in its view appeared to be doing the same, with massive columns and stone walls changing position slightly.

Then he realized what it was.

"Switch to Camera Five!"

Laura tapped at the display and the image changed to show an angle from the south side of the find, nearest the shore, looking down the slope of the ruins, down the side of the volcano.

And everything was moving.

Away from the camera.

Reading peered over their shoulders. "What's happening?"

But Acton couldn't answer. It was simply too horrible to voice. Laura saved him.

"It's-it's all sliding deeper."

Finally, the camera they were watching began to slide with the ancient city, then tumble as the tripod lost its footing. Suddenly everything went blank as the relay was pulled out of range, too deep for its signal to reach the surface.

And perhaps ending any chance mankind had of proving once and for all whether Atlantis had ever existed.

"Is it lost?" asked Spencer.

Acton closed his eyes, nodding slowly. "I think so."

"Surely you can still find it. I mean, you know where it is."

Acton turned back toward their vehicle, filled with pessimism. "It depends on how far it slid, and if it was buried. If it went beyond dive depth, then only submersibles will be able to reach it, and if it was buried, it could take years, even decades, to find it." He sighed. "If ever."

Spencer snorted. "Give James Cameron a call. He'll find it and make a movie out of it."

His father gave him a look. "Now's not the time."

Spencer's face sagged. "Sorry."

Acton forced a smile, patting the young man on the shoulder. "It's okay, perhaps a little humor is what we need right now. We still have the footage from the cameras, and it's all stored safely in the cloud, and we still have…" His jaw dropped. "The trident! What happened to the trident?"

Reading's eyes narrowed. "That giant fork you were talking about?"

"Yes. We left it on our boat when we were diving, but we were captured. We need to find that boat! That trident could be the only thing left that proves Atlantis might exist!"

Reading frowned. "I'm afraid I've got bad news on that front. I talked to the owner of the dive shop, and he said they had to go out and retrieve your boat."

Acton wanted to look at his friend with some inkling of hope, but there was no point. "And the trident?"

"He said it had been picked clean."

Acton's shoulders slumped, his eyes burning as Laura fell into his arms, as crushed as he was. "So somewhere, out there, is the only proof that Atlantis ever existed."

EQ Hotel & Casino
Shanghai, China

Kane walked into the hotel's restaurant, Tien on his arm, and strode toward Zhang's table, the thin man enjoying his breakfast with several of the high-priced talent on display the night before. "Good morning, Mr. Zhang."

Zhang looked up at him, his eyes darting toward Tien for a moment. "Ahh, Mr. Kane. I trust you had an enjoyable evening."

Kane lifted Tien's hand and gave it a gentle kiss. "A wonderful time, thank you."

Zhang motioned to two empty chairs. "Please, join me."

Kane pulled out a chair for Tien, then pushed it in for her before sitting. "I have excellent news for you, Mr. Zhang."

Zhang paused. "Oh?"

"We have found your yacht."

Zhang's eyebrows shot up, a smile spreading. "That *is* good news!" He paused. "Where?"

"Macao."

Zhang's eyes narrowed. "Someone actually thought they could steal my yacht, my *custom* built yacht, and sail it into Macao?"

Kane leaned back in his chair, putting his arm around Tien's shoulders. "Which is why my company has its suspicions."

Zhang put down his fork, clearly not pleased. "Oh?"

"Yes, they feel this may have been an attempt at insurance fraud on your part. We pay you for the yacht, then you sell it, or, perhaps even more boldly, reclaim it without telling us."

Zhang's cheeks burned red. "You dare accuse me!"

Kane laughed, dismissing the anger with a wave of his hand. "As I said, my *company* has its suspicions. *I*, on the other hand, have none." He leaned forward, the flushed cheeks waning. "I'll tell you *my* theory, and it's the one that will go in the official report."

"I'm all ears."

Kane smiled, Zhang's ears prominent. "My theory is that a rival, or perhaps merely a local gang, stole your yacht, with the intention of selling it. When they reached their buyers in Macao, they realized it was simply too unique to sell. Your yacht did not exactly come off an assembly line."

Zhang leaned back, a slight smile on his face, the yarn being spun apparently to his satisfaction. "No, it definitely is not."

"Exactly. Which is why I think once they realized they had stolen something that could never be sailed by a new buyer, they abandoned it." Kane leaned forward slightly, removing his arm from Tien's shoulders. "So, my final report will indicate that you were the victim here, that your property was recovered, and nothing untoward happened."

Zhang smiled broadly. "This is good news." He stood, extending his hand across the table. Kane rose, shaking it. "If you ever need anything, Mr. Kane, I am at your service."

"I'm glad you said that." He placed a hand on Tien's shoulder and smiled at her. "I find I am quite taken by your gift to me." He turned to Zhang. "I would consider all debts paid if you were to give her to me."

Zhang's jaw dropped slightly, his eyes widening as he sat back into his chair. Then he laughed, holding out his hand toward Tien. *"This? This* is what you ask of me, when you could have asked for almost anything?"

Kane bowed slightly. "I am a man of simple tastes."

Zhang laughed, flicking his wrist at Tien, Kane's steadying hand unable to halt her trembling. "Fine, take her. I have a dozen more."

Kane bowed even deeper. "Thank you. And one more thing?"

Zhang's smiled eased slightly. "Yes?"

"Nobody ever touches her, or her family."

The smile disappeared as Zhang realized what was actually going on. "Agreed."

"Thank you."

"And Mr. Kane?"

"Yes?"

"I better never see you, or her, again."

Baltasar Residence

Pico Island, Azores

Baltasar leaned back in his chair, a good fire roaring to his left, taking the edge off the chilly night. There had been a lot of excitement on his beach for a couple of weeks, there even rumors of some great archaeological find just off the coast, though the fact the scientists had left yesterday, made him suspect it was nothing.

But that didn't matter. He'd be playing it up on the Internet for years to come. The more fools that thought they'd find ancient treasure under the water, the more that would rent equipment from his shop.

Then again, maybe it wasn't all nonsense.

He stared over at the mantle of his fireplace, his hard work over the past few days worth it, the artifact he had found stowed on the scientists' boat when they abandoned it, now a beautiful, brilliant gold. Some might have thought of it as stealing, but not him. As far as he was concerned, it was compensation for the trouble he had been forced to go through, and the risk they had put his boat in. Boats were expensive, and so was insurance, which he didn't bother with.

He stared at it, searching for the proper name, something he hadn't been able to do since the Internet had been cut off.

Maybe Erasmo will know.

He'd be seeing him for drinks after dinner, and he'd try to remember to ask the man without giving away his secret.

His cellphone beeped by his side and he checked the display, a smile spreading from a surge of excitement as he started to get a flood of messages from the mainland, service apparently at least partially restored. He fired off a text message to Erasmo, canceling their plans.

And asking him what the name was for a giant fork.

Pier #6, Canal #4

Atlantis

The fall

Ampheres came to a halt, his hands on his knees, hunched over as he gasped for breath. He and Mestor were at the outer ring now, the pattern of canals cut into the landscape creating wide swaths of lands the farther from the core one went. It meant less citizenry, as agriculture, factories, and fish plants filled the area, but there was nothing that could shield them from the horrors occurring behind them.

The mountain was erupting with flowing red-hot fluid as dark clouds, bursting from the top, spread out and filled the sky, blotting out the sun, bolts of lightning streaking across the underside of the thick undulating mass—a terrifying spectacle if there ever was one.

"Hurry, Professor, we're almost there."

Ampheres nodded, forcing himself upright by sheer will alone, the only thing keeping him going, the knowledge his family awaited. At the moment, he couldn't care less about leading the students on board the vessel into a brave new future. He just wanted to hug his wife and children.

"Ampheres!"

He stared ahead and saw his wife waving from the deck of the large research vessel, and he breathed a sigh of relief, his body providing him a surge of energy as he sprinted past Mestor. He raced across a plank leading to the boat, Mestor on his heels, and two students immediately pulled it aboard.

"Let's go!" shouted Mestor, and a group of students sprang into action, lines freed from the dock and sails raised, the boat underway within moments of boarding.

But all that went unnoticed by Ampheres as he held his wife and children, all sobbing with fear and relief.

"I was so worried you weren't going to make it!"

He squeezed his wife tighter. "So was I." He stared up at the sails, flapping overhead, the boat pulling away from the dock. Dozens of smaller boats were making their way toward the sea, but the numbers were pitiable.

And all but a handful would have no hope of navigating the seas, and even if they did, they likely lacked the provisions for such a journey.

We may actually be the only ones to survive.

The water rippled and the shoreline trembled as the rumble of another earthquake tore through the city, buildings in the distance collapsing as if mere children's toys, knocked aside by a toddler's swept hand.

Then the most horrific sight had them all gasping, even those manning the boat pausing for a moment to see. It was the Obelisk of Atlantis, the monument that marked the center of their city, where the ten kings had united eons ago to lay the foundation of what would become the most advanced civilization of the known world.

And it was no more.

Its ten stories of stone, topped by a massive torch encased in reflective stone, that stood as a beacon to vessels at sea at night, was cracked at its midpoint, the top half sliding to the ground and out of sight, a cloud of dust billowing up from behind the buildings that blocked their view.

If there were any that doubted this was the end, if they had witnessed what they just had, their doubts could be no more.

"Wait!"

Ampheres peered into the darkness and saw a woman sprinting along the canal, waving at them. He frowned as his chest tightened. They were likely only provisioned for an exact number, and if they took more on board, it could risk the entire mission. He closed his eyes as they burned with the knowledge that this was but the first of what would probably be many difficult decisions in the days and years ahead, and if he couldn't make this one call, there would be no hope for any of them.

"We have to save her," sobbed his wife. "She's just one. We have plenty of room."

The students all stared at him, and he felt faint. He sucked in a breath, holding it for a moment before exhaling. "We cannot save anyone but ourselves. There aren't enough supplies, and if we stop for one, we risk being overwhelmed with more."

The students seem relieved that a decision had been made, one they apparently agreed with. He turned to his wife who stared at him in horror, and it made him feel as if for the first time in her life, she were looking at him as less of a man, and it had his stomach tying itself in knots.

"Please, wait! Professor Gadeiros sent me!"

Ampheres spun toward the woman, now beside the boat, appearing to be nearing the point of exhaustion. He turned to the man operating the tiller. "Get closer!"

"Yes, sir!"

He pushed to the right, the boat steering slightly to the left, nearing the edge of the canal. The woman suddenly leaped through the air and reached out for the side of the boat. She slammed into the hull, her hands gripping the edge as several of the students rushed over, pulling her on board. She lay on the deck for a few moments, her stomach expanding and contracting as she caught her breath, then held up a hand, one of the students hauling her to her feet.

"Who are you?" asked Ampheres as he stepped forward. "Are you one of the professor's students?"

She shook her head. "No, I'm Senior Enforcer Kleito."

Ampheres tensed and took a step back. "What do you want?"

She raised a hand. "I'm not here for you, Professor Ampheres. Not anymore." She pointed at the devastation behind them. "We have to stop this."

Ampheres stared at her for a moment, his eyes narrowing. "I'm not sure I understand. There's no way to stop this. Surely you know that."

She dismissed his words with a violent shake of her head, the woman clearly convinced of the possibility of doing the impossible. "You don't understand. This can all be stopped. I just need the trident!"

His eyes shot wide open. "You don't think—"

"The gods are angry at us! They're destroying us for having lost faith, for having tossed them aside. Your theft of Poseidon's Trident was the final straw. The disrespect you showed finally forced them to act. If I return it to its resting place, and the people put their faith back in the gods, we can stop all this. Surely they'll forgive us!"

Ampheres wasn't certain what to say. The woman was clearly mad, though he didn't blame her. It was to be expected that some would turn to superstition in these desperate hours, but the notion that returning an artifact handed down over the generations as a symbol of defying the gods and tossing off past superstitions, could somehow placate imaginary beings into stopping their wanton destruction, was laughable. She pulled a baton from her belt, gripping it menacingly.

"Give me the trident, Professor. All our lives depend on it."

He held up his hands, taking another step back. "I understand you're scared. We all are. But nothing can save them. It's over."

She advanced toward him.

"Even if I believed you, it doesn't matter. I don't have the trident."

She stopped, her jaw dropping, confusion on her face as this was apparently not a contingency she had planned on. "You-you don't have it?" Her shoulders slumped, her head drooping forward as all will seemed to leave her.

"Umm, Professor?"

Ampheres turned to one of the students. "Yes?"

"Sir, we have the trident here. We brought it with your family."

An insane sense of hope surged through him for a moment, as if the woman's crazed beliefs might actually be of sound mind, and he beckoned at the young man. "Bring it to her, quickly!"

The man disappeared below decks for a moment, then returned with the trident, still wrapped in the cloth Mestor had hidden it in earlier that day. Kleito stared at it, her eyes wide, then grabbed it from the student, quickly unwrapping it, gasping as the brilliant golden trident, something every school child saw at least once while learning the history of their great civilization, was revealed.

She turned to Ampheres, her wide eyes filled with the hope that had already left him. "Thank you!"

He smiled at her as one might a child, pity filling him as he regarded the naïve woman. "What will you do?" He pointed. "We've cleared the canals."

She handed the trident to the student then quickly stripped down to her undergarments. "I can make it. I have to!" She grabbed the trident then leaped over the stern and into the sea that surrounded the island, swimming back toward their doomed city using only one arm, struggling with the weight of the relic. Ampheres stared after her, willing her to succeed, only so that she might survive a little while longer, filled with hope.

But it was a useless endeavor.

As the boat continued to put distance between them and the island, the cries of desperation and screams of terror continued to carry over the waves, hundreds of boats of varying sizes now filling the waters, giving Ampheres a hint of hope that perhaps more would survive than just the fifty some souls aboard this craft.

When suddenly all hope was lost.

A cracking sound unlike anything he could possibly imagine filled the air, and he felt his wife grip his hand tightly as she came up beside him.

"Oh no!"

He didn't see what had her concerned at first, perhaps because he wasn't willing to see it, perhaps because he couldn't fathom what he was witnessing. The entire city was tilting toward them, slowly rising into the air, almost imperceptibly at first, but as each moment passed, it became more obvious what was happening.

He searched the sea for Kleito, to shout a warning, but couldn't find her, the poor woman probably already drowned. Yet it wouldn't matter. His eyes were irresistibly drawn to the horror unfolding, the crew of students joining them at the stern of the ship, their duties forgotten, as they witnessed the final, complete destruction of everything they had ever known.

In a manner Ampheres had never considered possible.

The greatest city ever created by man, the legendary Atlantis, was slipping into the sea, consumed by the oceans that had protected it from outside invaders, the very ocean that had allowed it to flourish for millennia, dedicating the resources of its people to self-improvement rather than war, to science rather than superstition, to love of life rather than greed and want.

His chest ached and his tears flowed freely as they stared in silence, the city tilted at an unimaginable angle, sliding out of sight, the screams and cries of his fellow citizens silenced.

Leaving nothing behind but those in the boats.

"What's happening?"

Ampheres stared into the darkness of what once was, trying to make sense of what one of the students had noticed first. It was some sort of gaping hole in the water, where the city had once been.

"The sea is sinking as well!" cried someone, and Ampheres leaned forward, still trying to understand.

Then it all made sense.

The water was rushing to fill the void created by the missing land that had once been their home, and as the water surged into the empty expanse that had been the island, now reduced to the mountain still spewing destruction, a massive wave had been created—or perhaps that wasn't it.

Perhaps it wasn't a wave.

Yet it didn't matter what it was.

The screams from the boats still closer to what had been the shore, were his first clue of the impending doom as the smaller craft began to be dragged into the void, easily dozens of stories deep, disappearing from sight as the first tugs of inevitability were felt on their own craft.

He spun, looking up at the sails, still full, but useless. "Everybody hang on!" He dropped to his knees, as did his wife, and he wrapped his arm around a rung of the gunwale, then gripped his wife and children. "I love you."

His wife was sobbing, her eyes red, her cheeks stained from the tears and the salt of the sea, yet she said nothing for a moment, too terrified to speak. "I love you too."

He hugged her hard as the boat tipped, gaining speed in the wrong direction. He held his children tight to him as they screamed. "Close your eyes!" He squeezed his own shut, and for the first time in his life, he prayed to the gods, decades of faith in science, rather than religion, thrust aside, as Poseidon took His revenge on the arrogant Atlanteans who had dared question His power over them.

THE END

ACKNOWLEDGEMENTS

The concept for this book came from an idea I had of Niner walking out of the water and tossing an artifact on the beach, then declaring, "Hey, I think I just found Atlantis." I thought it was a hilarious idea, and I was determined to figure out a way to bring this to life. The problem was how to tie the history and present day. That was solved through a dream—yup, a dream. I had the idea of somebody from Atlantis stealing an object, and it was that object that was later found thousands of years later. By focusing on the object, I didn't need to link people into the equation, and then have descendants of Atlantis come knocking on Acton's door. By focusing on stumbling upon the plot to blow up the undersea cables, it made the perpetrators the bad guys, rather than, again, Atlanteans.

The final challenge was Atlantis itself. Since there's no proof it ever actually existed, authors throughout history have written a wide range of things about it, and with the exception of the awesome Stargate Atlantis TV series, I haven't read any of these other accounts. I was certain, however, that I didn't want to write some science fiction version of Atlantis, yet I still wanted them to be more advanced than those civilizations surrounding them at the time. I had the epiphany of making them culturally advanced, rather than technologically advanced, though I did have a little fun with creative use of water power.

I hope you enjoyed my spin on Atlantis. The scenario laid out is plausible, and it does make you wonder what curiosities could be buried under the sea that have been lost for thousands of years, or perhaps far longer than that!

As usual, there are people to thank. My dad for all the research, Fred Newton for some nautical info, Bob Blizzard for some Goose Bay help, Brent Richards for some weapons help, Isabelle Laprise-Enright, Marianne Hossler, Jamie Waughtel, Amish Parekh, and Bob Eager for their suggestions for character names in the Facebook contest, and, as usual, my wife, daughter, and mother, as well as the launch team.

I'd like to take a moment also to thank my proofing team. I was very ill around the end of this process, and things were delayed to where there were literally only days remaining before the deadline. My proofing team came through for me, and I'd like to take the time to specifically thank Fred Newton, Malcolm Stone, Chuck Arnold, Sheelagh Rogers, Tony Daugherty, and Charlene Klasen for helping me meet the deadline.

To those who have not already done so, please visit my website at www.jrobertkennedy.com then sign up for the Insider's Club to be notified of new book releases. Your email address will never be shared or sold, and you'll only receive the occasional email from me, as I don't have time to spam you!

Thank you once again for reading.